Wild Passion

Wilder Irish, book 1

Mari Carr

ISBN: 978-1-950870-07-3

Editor: Kelli Collins

Cover artist: Melissa Gill Designs

Print formatting: Mari Carr

Dedication

This book is dedicated to Lexi Blake, who very kindly sat me down in a bar one night and said, "You know, it's time for a next generation Wild Irish."

And that was all she wrote…

Prologue

"Tell me the story again, Pop Pop. The one about my name."

Patrick smiled at the dark-haired child, his beloved granddaughter. "Och. You've heard that story a thousand times, my sweet. Wouldn't you rather hear me sing?"

The little girl giggled and shook her head emphatically. It had become a running joke between Patrick and Caitlyn that she considered his singing voice very poor.

"Are you sure?" he teased. "You don't want to hear my *Irish Lullaby*?" He started to sing, only getting as far as "Too-ra-loo," when she covered her ears.

"No. The story. The story! About me."

Patrick's daughter, Keira, had given him the what-for the first time he'd told Caitlyn the old folktale, insisting that it was a bit too heavy for a four-year-old. Regardless, Caitlyn loved the tale and had since asked to hear it countless times.

"Fine, fine. But first, let's get you under the covers."

He was babysitting his young grandchildren while Keira and Will went out for the evening. They'd had a rare chance for a date night, something that didn't come along often now that they had two wee ones at home.

Caitlyn's baby brother, Lochlan, was already fast asleep in his crib, and given the sleepy look in her eyes, Caitlyn wouldn't last much longer either.

Caitlyn snuggled beneath her *Beauty and the Beast* comforter, the beautiful princess in a bright yellow dress dancing in the arms of the beast. Earlier in the evening, Patrick had spun Caitlyn around in the same manner as she insisted he play the beast.

Apart from the muted glow coming from the bedside lamp, the only other light in the room was produced from the small aquarium on top of Caitlyn's dresser. A bright blue fish swam around the tiny tank. It wasn't unusual for a child growing up in Baltimore to become enamored of fish, considering the fine aquarium the city held.

"Well, as you know," Patrick began, "your name is actually a nickname for Cathleen, and oh, wasn't she a bonny woman in this story? There came such a time that two evil men appeared in Ireland. They were on a mission from the devil."

Caitlyn's eyes grew wide at this point in the story, as they always did. The young girl was a sucker for a scary story. "The devil is bad."

"Indeed he is. And at the time, there was a famine. What did I tell you a famine was?"

"Everybody was hungry because there wasn't any macaroni and cheese. Or chicken nuggets."

Patrick nodded and grinned. She was a bright little thing, who couldn't conceive of a world that didn't contain Kraft Macaroni & Cheese. Patrick couldn't fault her terror of such an occurrence. Though his daughter Riley—whose homemade mac and cheese could win awards—would have a fit if he confessed it, he was fond of the bright orange box stuff himself.

"I feel bad for the hungry little kids in that town. Their tummies must've hurt."

Patrick didn't doubt for a moment his tiny Cait was destined to do great things. In addition to her intelligence, she had compassion in spades. "That's right. They were very hungry and they wished they could have some of that macaroni and cheese you gobbled up for your supper."

"Gobble. Gobble." Caitlyn mimicked a turkey and giggled, as he continued the tale.

"So the devil sent these two bad men to make a deal with the hungry Irish. They could trade their souls in exchange for gold."

"And then they'd be rich and they could eat all the Happy Meals they wanted," she added.

"That's right. But was that a good thing for the poor people to do?"

She shook her head earnestly. "No. It's bad to give your soul to the devil because he's a big meanie."

"That's right." Patrick had brushed over some of the finer details of the story, but he suspected as Caitlyn got older, she'd eventually start asking questions about the tale, seeking a deeper understanding of it all. For now, she was happy to know there were bad guys and...

"But did Cathleen sell her soul to the devil?"

Caitlyn shouted out an excited, "No! Because she was good."

"And very smart," Patrick added.

Caitlyn loved the idea that she was the heroine in the story. The one destined to save everyone. "Say what she did," she urged.

"When Cathleen realized what the hungry people were doing, she went to the bad men and said she would give them her soul in exchange for those of the whole town."

"Because the devil wanted her soul the most. On account of her being the best. She saved them all."

Patrick nodded. "That's right. She did. And because her actions were so brave, so selfless, she was rewarded."

"The devil didn't get her soul because God swooped down and grabbed it and he took her to heaven and she got to sit on the clouds with the angels and eat chocolate cake and ice cream all the time."

Patrick chuckled at how much Caitlyn embellished the tale with each retelling. The last time, the courageous Cathleen had gotten to sing and dance and eat peanut butter and jelly sandwiches, so clearly heaven changed according to whatever Caitlyn fancied at the time.

"That's right," he confirmed. "She saved all the hungry Irish and was rewarded. With cake and ice cream."

Caitlyn's body relaxed as they came to the end of the story. Patrick rose from his perch on the side of her bed, bending down to kiss her forehead.

"Pop Pop," she said, her voice going thick with the sleep that was coming to claim her quickly.

"Yes, my little Caitie-bug?"

"One day I'm going to save the poor Irish, and when I do, I'll share my cake and ice cream with them so they aren't hungry."

Patrick ran the backs of his fingers along her soft cheek. "Ah, lass. I know you will. Because you're smart and brave and kind."

He gave her another kiss on the brow, turned on her starfish nightlight near the door and left the room, silently praying to live a long life. He was looking forward to watching his fierce granddaughter save the Irish.

Chapter One

"Jesus. What's he doing in here?"

Caitlyn Wallace looked around the pub, searching for someone who could have caught her cousin Colm's eye.

Seeing no one of interest, she turned her gaze back to Colm. "He who?"

"Lucas Whiting."

While Caitlyn didn't have a clue what Lucas Whiting looked like, she sure as hell knew his name. The Whitings were to Baltimore what the Kennedys were to Martha's Vineyard. There was precious little property of value in the city that the Whitings didn't have some vested interest in.

"He's here?"

Colm nodded, and then used the upswing of his chin to direct her attention to a table near the back of the pub. Three men in expensive power suits sat together, drinking pints of Guinness. She assumed the one in the center was Lucas. He was older than the other two, with gray hair, serious eyes and deep frown grooves around his mouth that told her he didn't smile much. If ever.

"Looks the type of a gazillionaire, doesn't he?" she said.

Colm turned his head, his look quizzical. "You think? I always thought he looked more like a rugby player."

Caitlyn turned back to the table. Clearly she'd focused on the wrong man. Once she'd spotted the older guy, she'd stopped looking. "Which one is he?"

"Man on the right," Colm replied before walking toward the bar. He claimed a stool and started talking to his dad, Caitlyn's Uncle Tris, who was manning the bar.

Rather than join him, Caitlyn remained near the entrance, so she could check out the man on the right.

"Oh," she breathed.

Colm had the right of it. Lucas was built much larger and broader and more muscular than she would have pictured him. For some reason, she'd imagined a more elegant, sophisticated, clean-shaven, well-dressed, paper-pushing wimp. Lucas Whiting resembled a thug, with his wide shoulders and scruffy beard that was pushing the five-o'clock-shadow deal by a few days. He looked like the kind of guy who'd been in more than a few fistfights. He also struck her as the type who'd most likely won every single one.

Originally, her gaze hadn't landed on him for more than a split second because her mind had seen that build and thought "bodyguard."

"Can you believe he's back here again?"

Caitlyn glanced over at her cousin Ailis, who was waiting the tables at the pub that night.

"Who?" Caitlyn wondered if she'd missed a step somewhere.

"Lucas Whiting."

"He's been here before?"

Ailis nodded. "Yeah. About a month or so ago. He chatted with Tris and Ewan about selling the pub. They laughed and told him he was wasting his time. He left and I think we all thought that was the end of it."

"Why didn't I know about this?"

Ailis grinned as Caitlyn trailed behind her, so her cousin could deliver the drinks she'd been carrying. "I suspect you were knee-deep in a case. Besides, you've been in workaholic mode this past year since you and Sammy split. It's rare to get your total attention."

Caitlyn didn't bother to argue that point. It was true. Sammy had accused her of living inside her head. Tried to use that as a reason for cheating on her. The stupid asshole.

Her gaze returned to Lucas Whiting's table. He was no longer conversing with the men sitting with him. Instead, he was studying the bar, his sharp, dark eyes taking in everything around him.

Caitlyn did the same, trying to imagine what Lucas was thinking. For a second, she heard the lines to that classic Billy Joel number "Piano Man" in her head. While it was a Friday night—not Saturday—the regular crowd had certainly shuffled in. The place was booming.

Hunter Maxwell, one of their current singers, was on stage with his guitar and harmonica setup. He was super talented, and Caitlyn knew that was one reason the place was so crowded.

Hunter was destined for stardom. She was as sure of that as she was that Hunter had it bad for Ailis. Ailis, however, seemed oblivious to that fact. Or she was ignoring it. Having grown up being homeschooled on a tour bus as Sky and Teagan rocked the world with their music for the first eighteen years of her life, Ailis was determined to live her adult years in a house without wheels. Problem was Hunter wanted the wheels, the big bus and the different-city-every-night stardom Ailis's parents enjoyed.

Caitlyn turned her attention away from the stage. Uncle Tris was manning the bar, talking football with Pop Pop, who sat on "his" stool at the center of the long mahogany counter, surrounded by his cronies—some nearly, but not quite, as old as him.

Most of her friends were amazed when she told them her grandfather was ninety-two years old. He had the energy and health of someone two decades younger. He claimed it was his family that kept him going, gave him a reason to keep chugging along. Aunt Riley always said the truth of it was he was too nosy to depart this earth before he got to see how all his grandkids turned out. Which was why Riley was convinced he'd outlive them all. Caitlyn sincerely hoped that was true. She couldn't imagine a world without Pop Pop.

"Does Pop Pop know about the offer?" Caitlyn asked.

Ailis shook her head. "No. Like I said, they turned it down and the guy went away. Since it was a nonissue, they decided not to bother Pop Pop with it."

"Good. I'd hate for him to worry about this. Although, it doesn't look like it's a nonissue anymore."

"I know. Riley said he'd be back. After all, the Whitings have been snatching up quite a bit of property in this area. Ewan seemed to think they'd convinced him they wouldn't sell, for any price, but now..."

Given the dark, threatening looks Tris was throwing Lucas's way, it was obvious her uncle was on the defensive, ready to defend the bar to the death. Not that he'd have to take up that battle alone.

She caught sight of Ewan and Riley standing just on the other side of the large opening between Pat's Pub and Sunday's Side, the restaurant named for Caitlyn's grandmother, giving Lucas the same evil eye.

One of the perks of being a member of a large family was there were never less than twenty people who had your back. Lucas Whiting would have been smart to take the original rejection and move on.

As she considered that, she looked back toward him and discovered he was staring at her. She held his gaze for a moment, and then glanced away. It was no good. She still felt the weight of his eyes on her.

"Do you know Lucas Whiting?" Ailis asked.

Caitlyn shook her head as she faced her cousin. "No. Why?"

"Because he's staring at you. Big time."

Caitlyn forced herself to look back. And sure enough, Ailis was telling the truth. Whatever study he'd been doing of the pub appeared to have ended with her.

She felt the inexplicable need to escape that heavy gaze. It unnerved her. And, well, dammit, it turned her on. She experienced an arousal she hadn't felt in months. No, strike that. A year.

Caitlyn worked hard to put that uneasy feeling away. It wasn't a state she wanted to dwell on. After Sammy's betrayal, she'd decided to take a year off from dating to recover from her broken heart and focus on her career, get her priorities straight. She had stayed with Sammy for all the wrong reasons.

Actually, just two wrong reasons.

The first was the same one that had existed in all her previous long-term relationships. Love. Caitlyn wanted it. Desperately. She longed for a relationship like her parents had, or any of her aunts and uncles. She wanted to come home every night to the one person who made life worth living.

And she wanted that so badly, she'd tried to force Sammy into that role, tried to convince herself that what they shared was a great and lasting love. Just like she had with Matt and Brad and...

Every single time one of her relationships failed, she was forced to face the fact that she'd fallen for the wrong man again. One who didn't love her as much as she loved him or who wasn't as committed toward building a life with her.

The other reason she'd hung in there too long with Sammy was at least unique from her other relationships. The sex. It had been great. So much so, she'd tricked herself into believing that the rest of their relationship was fine. When it wasn't. She had that truth knocked into her when she'd come home early and found him boinking the middle school music teacher who lived across the hall.

Caitlyn had packed her bags and moved into the apartment above her family's business, Pat's Pub, where she shared the spacious space with six of her ten cousins. Riley had taken to referring to the second floor as the Collins Dorm after several of the cousins moved in, and the name stuck.

She tried to stifle a yawn. Her family was going to have to deal with Lucas Whiting on their own. It had been a damn long day. "I'm beat. Think I'll go upstairs and relax for a little while."

After law school, she'd opted to work in the public sector as opposed to pursuing a job with a big firm. She'd started as an attorney with Baltimore Legal Aid, a nonprofit firm that provided free legal services to low-income people, working her ass off for very little pay, while gaining experience.

Then, once her cousin Colm graduated from law school too, they opened their own practice, the Collins Law Firm. While it was Colm's last name as well, the name of the firm was actually a nod to their beloved Pop Pop, who was so proud of them with their "big, fancy law degrees," as he referred to them, that he fairly burst from the emotion.

For the past five years, she and Colm had worked long hours in an attempt to build a name for their firm. Caitlyn specialized in services for seniors, serving on a local committee that worked to keep older citizens not only in their homes, but to ensure they were living in safe environments. Colm's specialty was in family and children's services.

Their firm had acquired a reputation for wheeling and dealing on payment. Which basically meant they only charged what their clients could afford to pay. Her mom, Keira, claimed she and Colm reminded her of old-school doctors, trading their services for eggs or a fat hog. Caitlyn had always laughed at that description—until a couple months earlier, when Colm had literally accepted freshly caught trout and a bottle of homemade moonshine as a payment. Then she realized things had gotten out of hand. Not that they'd change their policy. They had just as many clients who could afford to pay as those who couldn't, so it wasn't like they were starving. Besides, poor people deserved good legal help as much as the rich.

"Are you going to come back down later?" Ailis asked.

Caitlyn shrugged. Ailis was worried about her. Actually, the whole Collins clan was. Her entire family had managed to pull her aside at some point over the past few months to talk to her about her all-work, no-play lifestyle and how it wasn't healthy. They weren't telling her anything she didn't know, but she was finding it too hard to break the pattern.

At first, work had been a salve to her wounds. Now, it was all she could remember how to do. She was too afraid to look for love, or even just sex. Her relationship with Sammy had been a disaster. Shit, her last three long-term love affairs had ended badly, each one leaving her with a broken heart.

She was starting to get trigger shy. Maybe she wasn't cut out for marriage and happily ever after. Of course, every time that thought crossed her mind, she felt like crying, so she tucked it away again.

"Caitlyn," her cousin began.

"If I don't fall asleep on the couch, I'll be back down in an hour or so." Caitlyn vowed to try to keep that promise, but she was dog-tired, weary to the bone, and in no mood to be around people or noise or—

She groaned softly.

Sammy walked into the pub.

"Seriously?" she muttered. "Fuck my life."

Fortunately, he hadn't spotted her yet.

Ailis groaned. "Jesus, he's thick. If Uncle Tris spots him, he's a dead man. I'll run interference while you escape."

Since "the one time he ever cheated on her," Sammy had called, texted, and hounded her on social media to beg for her forgiveness. At first, she'd told him to fuck off. Then she'd blocked him on everything. When he realized he couldn't get to her through the regular channels, the dumbass had actually Venmo'ed her twenty bucks because he realized he could send her a long message with the money. She'd pocketed the cash, deleted the message without reading it and threatened to slap a restraining order on him if he didn't leave her alone.

That had been four months ago. She'd thought the threat had been enough because he'd been quiet since then.

Caitlyn nodded her thanks and headed toward the back of the pub, to the door that led to the stairs to the second floor. She'd nearly made a clean getaway when her path was blocked. By a very large, broad, power-suited chest.

She didn't bother to look up. She knew who was standing in her way. "Excuse me."

She tried to sidestep Lucas Whiting, but he followed her direction, not allowing her to pass. She flashed him an angry look.

"I said excuse me." While most of her cases were settled in conference rooms, on occasion, deals couldn't be struck. Which meant she was no stranger to courtrooms. As such, she was the master of many tones. She could sound conciliatory or infuriated or sympathetic—whatever she thought would be most effective on the judge or jury. Right now, her tone was pure irritation.

"I apologize." His face didn't match his words. He wasn't sorry. He also wasn't a thug. She'd only had a distant view of him from across the room. Up close, Lucas Whiting fell into a category she'd never created before. In a world of hot or not, Lucas sort of straddled the line. He was handsome, but terrifying. Attractive, but intense. Every pleasant feature on his face seemed marred by something she could only think to call power…or maybe it was hunger.

His deep-set midnight-colored eyes were too sharp, too focused for her to enjoy the hue. His chiseled jaw appeared to be clenched just a smidge too tightly. And she wondered if he kept the beard as a way to hide his far-too-serious face rather than as a fashion statement. Maybe he thought it made him less intimidating. She almost laughed aloud at that thought. The man was intimidation incarnate.

"I was wondering if you would like to join me for a drink."

Of course. Obviously, Whiting knew who she was. Granddaughter of the owner.

The asshole probably thought he could pour a couple glasses of wine into her and have her spilling all the family secrets.

"No, thank you. I was just leaving."

He frowned as he glanced behind him. Then he pointed toward the front. "The exit is that way."

It was on the tip of her tongue to say, "And my home is that way," but his confusion caught her unaware.

Maybe he *didn't* know who she was.

"Yes. But..." Caitlyn debated how to play this. If Lucas didn't know who she was, perhaps she could employ the same plan she'd suspected he was using on her. She could join him for a drink, draw him into a conversation about the pub and see what his intentions were.

Before she could figure out the best way to go, Sammy found her.

"There you are."

Caitlyn turned at the sound of her ex's voice, Lucas Whiting forgotten in an instant. "Do you have some sort of death wish?"

"It's been months, Caitie."

"Don't call me that."

"Caitlyn," Sammy quickly corrected, as if his reticence would work on her.

She'd hit her limit with the idiot. "I'm filing the paperwork for a restraining order in the morning."

Sammy blanched. "You can't still be this mad at me. I've said I'm sorry a thousand times. And I am. God, Caitlyn. I've been kicking my own ass every night since you left. I screwed up. Big time. I know that. What we had…it was special. I miss you. I miss…" He paused, and she knew where he was heading.

Sex. He missed fucking her.

Wow, didn't that make her feel special?

"It's over between us, Sammy. I don't know how to say that to you any more clearly. Go back to Ms. Middle School Music."

Sammy shook his head rapidly. "No. No. I don't want her. She didn't get it. Didn't like," he swallowed loudly, "what *we* like."

Caitlyn flushed with anger, balling her fist. She'd never hit anyone before, but she was more than ready to kill him. "How dare you—"

"I think perhaps you should move on. The lady told you it's over."

Caitlyn was startled when Lucas decided to enter the conversation. She assumed he would move on at the first sign of Sammy's drama. For some strange reason, knowing he was there allowed her to calm down. While she was fairly certain her punch wouldn't leave a mark, Lucas Whiting looked the type to do some serious damage to Sammy. Which was exactly what *she* wanted.

"Who are you?" Sammy kept his tone fairly non-confrontational. Probably because he was smart enough to take one look at Lucas and know he wouldn't win in a physical fight against the man.

"I'll tell you who I am. I'm your worst nightmare if you don't get out of this pub and leave this woman alone."

Sammy blinked a couple times, no doubt trying to figure out if he'd heard what he thought he'd heard. Dumbass actually looked at her for help, and it took all the strength she had not to roll her eyes.

"Go home, Sammy. Don't come back."

The air seemed to seep out of him as Sammy held her gaze a second longer. And then, he turned to leave.

She twisted back toward Lucas, grinning despite her annoyance with basically everything at the moment. "What the hell was that? It was like you were channeling Liam Neeson or something for a second. I will find you. I'm your worst nightmare," she mimicked in a deep, deadly voice.

Lucas didn't look her way, didn't even acknowledge her joke. Instead, he continued to watch Sammy's retreating form.

Caitlyn saw her ex walk out of the pub. Then she glanced toward the bar. Very little happened that Uncle Tris didn't see or hear. He stared at her for a second. She gave him a covert wink to let him know she was fine. Regardless, his face remained stoic before he gave her a subtle nod.

He was going to leave her alone. For now. But she didn't fool herself into believing he wasn't going to be watching her like a hawk as long as she was talking to Lucas Whiting.

"Thank you for stepping in to help," she said, her gaze slipping to the door to her apartment. She was so close. To pajamas and a glass of wine and repeats of *Lucifer* on TV.

"Is my chivalry enough to convince you to join me for a drink?"

She glanced back at his table, surprised to find it unoccupied. "What happened to your friends?"

"They're business associates. And our meeting is over. They've gone home to their wives."

He gestured toward a chair and she gave in. Tiredness gave way to curiosity.

"No wife for you?"

He shook his head. "Would I invite you for a drink if there was?"

"The idiot you just kicked out of here was coming home to me after work. When he beat me there, he decided it would be a good idea to invite another woman to our bed. You'll forgive me if I'm not super trusting."

"I'm not married. Not engaged. Not living with or seriously dating anyone."

Caitlyn found herself trying to figure out Lucas's age. He had one of those faces that made it virtually impossible to guess. Not that she'd have to wonder for long. No doubt there was plenty of information about him on the Internet. She could discover that answer in one quick Google search on her phone.

"Divorced?" she asked.

"No."

She realized they'd sort of started this conversation in the middle, so she thought she'd try to drag them back a few steps to the beginning. "I'm Caitlyn Wallace, by the way."

His expression gave her no clue as to whether or not he recognized her name. If he'd done any research at all on the pub, he would have certainly come across her mother's name.

Pop Pop and her grandma Sunday had raised their seven children in the upstairs apartment Caitlyn was sharing with her cousins, in addition to running the pub and restaurant below. As they became adults, Tris took over the pub half of the business with Pop Pop while her mom, Keira Wallace, and Uncle Ewan ran Sunday's Side.

"Lucas Whiting."

"I know."

For the first time, she saw just the trace of a smile on his face. It made him appear almost human.

"The man who just left—"

"Sammy," she added.

"Former boyfriend or husband?"

"Ex-boyfriend. It's been a small consolation knowing that at least I was smart enough not to marry him."

"He asked?"

She shook her head. "Actually, no. He didn't."

Sammy was the last thing Caitlyn wanted to talk about tonight. Especially with Lucas Whiting. "Do you do a lot of business in pubs?"

Lucas lifted one shoulder casually. "Depends on the business."

Hello, Mr. Vague. She probed for more. "Okay. So what was tonight's pub-worthy business?"

"Real estate acquisition."

Fucker was good. He gave nothing away.

"Can I get you all something to drink?" Ailis was looking at Caitlyn curiously.

"I'll have another Guinness. Caitlyn?"

"I'll have the same. Thanks." She hoped her cousin wouldn't say anything to reveal her identity. The lawyer in her was determined to get to the truth in Lucas's short answers.

Ailis paused for just a second, but when Caitlyn didn't look at her or say more, she turned for the bar.

"I can't imagine there's much real estate left in Baltimore your family doesn't already own."

Lucas's gaze held hers intently. "There's always more to buy."

His response tweaked her for some reason.

"What if someone doesn't want to sell to you?"

His eyes narrowed the tiniest bit. Someone who was paying less attention wouldn't have even noticed, but Caitlyn had locked onto him. Her words had triggered something. Shit. She'd shown her hand. Revealed herself.

"Everyone has a price."

Her family didn't. Not when it came to this business. It wasn't just the Collins's livelihood. It was their home, their legacy to future generations. In some ways, the pub felt like the heartbeat of the family, the one thing that kept them all tied together.

"So no one has ever said no to you?"

For the first time, Lucas grinned. Caitlyn's response shook her. She was torn between running away from the hungry wolf and baring her neck to the beast.

Oh shit.

He leaned closer to her, his dark eyes penetrating, missing nothing. His expression seemed to say he knew she wouldn't say no to him.

Her pussy clenched, and she felt a trickle of wetness between her legs. What the hell was going on? Lucas shot one sexy freaking look at her and she was ready to tear off her clothes? It was definitely time to start dating again. Her hormones had decided to make a comeback...with a vengeance.

She tried to imagine what Lucas would look like without his shirt on. Did he have any tattoos? His thick, muscular arms seemed made for ink.

"What do you think?" he murmured.

About the tattoos? It took her a moment to stop undressing him with her eyes and recall her original question.

She'd asked if anyone ever said no to him.

"I don't know." She hated the almost breathless quality in her voice.

Her cheeks heated under his intense gaze, and she feared she was blushing. Lucas wasn't even bothering to hide his attraction to her. His eyes darted down to her breasts, and the shadow of his grin reappeared.

She averted her eyes when it became impossible to hide her own unwanted desires. Unfortunately, looking down only made it apparent that her nipples were poking through her blouse. They'd tightened the moment she sat down at the table and gotten a whiff of his musk cologne. Which meant Lucas knew exactly what effect he was having on her.

"People say no to me all the time, Caitlyn."

Her gaze lifted as she wondered if she would have the strength to deny him. In her mind, she could imagine him bidding her to strip, to kneel, to bend over the table. And she didn't doubt for a second she would comply. "People," she murmured. "Women?" The question slipped out unbidden.

Lucas parted his lips to speak, but she shook her head to cut him off.

"I didn't mean...never mind." She was babbling like an idiot. Time to get her shit together. "When people say no, when they turn down your offer, do you walk away?"

Lucas looked like he wanted to respond to her foolish slip of the tongue. She was grateful when she let her attempt to return them to safer ground stick. He tilted his head. "I never walk away. As I said, there's always a bottom line."

Caitlyn tried to recall the last time she'd felt this far out of her league. Years spent in her legal practice had honed her skills, her ability to stand up to even the most vicious of bullies. The problem was Lucas didn't strike her as a bully.

He felt more like—she swallowed heavily—a Dom.

And she was terrified he'd find a way to look deep inside her and see the one thing she really did *not* want Lucas Whiting to see.

Her mother had told her once that the worst thing a person could do was hide their true personality, to deny who they were, to try to conceal the one thing that made them beautiful, made them special.

Her mother knew who Caitlyn was. She knew it because they were the same underneath the skin. Mom had always seen, always tried to encourage Caitlyn in very subtle ways to accept her submissiveness. To embrace it and not view it as a weakness.

Caitlyn continually struggled with that acceptance, and she'd never had any difficulty keeping the trait hidden from pretty much everyone.

Until now.

The problem was Lucas was looking at her too closely. His body language, his carriage, the way he held himself, God, everything about him was luring her closer to the fire.

She pressed her legs together tightly, desperate to stop the sudden pulsing of her inner muscles that were screaming for sex. She needed to get a grip, needed to break free of...whatever this was. Lucas Whiting was the enemy, a threat to her family's livelihood. The thought of her family helped her find her bearings.

"I disagree about the bottom line. Some things simply can't be bought. For any price."

Lucas didn't bother to argue with her. His cool expression made it perfectly clear he thought he was right and she was wrong. His haughty attitude tweaked her.

"What do you do for a living, Caitlyn?"

"I'm a lawyer."

"Criminal or civil?"

"Civil. I have my own practice." She'd nearly said the name of her firm, but stopped short. Lucas might not recognize the name Wallace, but there was no way in hell he didn't know the Collins family owned this pub.

"Large firm?"

"No. Small. Just my cousin and I, though recently we've started putting out feelers, looking to expand, perhaps add another attorney or two."

"So business is good."

"Yes. It is. We work with lower-income families, senior citizens."

"I see."

"I primarily deal with property disputes, landlord and tenant issues, immigration. My cousin works more with divorce and child-custody type cases."

"So you're not ambulance chasers."

She shook her head and grinned. "No. We're not."

Ailis returned and placed their pints of beer on the table. Tris must have clued her cousin into the fact that Caitlyn was up to something, because she simply said she'd check on them in a bit and moved on to deliver drinks to the table next to them.

If they were counting on Caitlyn for information, they were going to be sorely disappointed. She was striking out. Big time.

She glanced toward the door to her apartment again. This game of cat and mouse had her on edge. And horny as hell.

She'd joined Lucas intent on discovering his secrets. Instead, it felt as if he was uncovering hers.

Caitlyn needed to move the conversation away from herself. Lucas was too good at dodging her questions, making her forget why he was here. "Was your meeting tonight successful? Were you able to buy what you wanted?"

"Not yet. We're in the beginning phases of the project."

"What does that involve?"

Lucas took a sip of beer and leaned back in his chair. "Research."

Caitlyn fought to control her temper—and the niggling bit of fear—his words provoked. He still wanted to buy Pat's Pub. There wasn't any doubt in her mind. What she couldn't tell was if he knew who she was, if he was baiting her, using her as part of that so-called research.

With her family's livelihood on the line, Caitlyn found herself better able to snuff out her ill-advised, unwanted attraction to Lucas. "Sounds like we're similar souls. I know quite a bit about research myself."

Her tone was more threatening than she'd intended, but she refused to cower, refused to let Lucas think he had the upper hand.

It was obvious her sudden aggression caught him off guard, making her think, once again, that he didn't have a clue who she was.

He recovered quickly. Damn him. "Tell me about yourself, Caitlyn."

She took a deep breath. Clearly, she still had a shot at trying to figure out his intentions. "I'm not sure what there is to tell. I think we pretty much covered all the bases already. I'm a lawyer. I'm single. And I have shitty taste in men."

Lucas chuckled, and she couldn't help but think it sounded rusty. Was this guy always so serious?

"I'm curious what the attraction was between you and Sammy. He doesn't seem like your type."

She frowned. "We've known each other approximately twenty minutes. How do you know what my type is?"

"You don't make it very far in my line of business without paying attention to details. You studied law. I study people."

Caitlyn felt compelled to push Lucas's buttons. The man seemed unshakable. Which made her long to rattle him. "You can't figure someone out in just twenty minutes."

"Sammy is weak."

She shrugged. "So?"

"So that's not what you want. What you need."

The way he said the word "need" had her chest going tight with fear...and, God help her, longing. "You have no idea what I need." She'd meant to put some power, some strength behind her assertion. Instead, the words came out in a whisper that belied them.

Once again, Lucas didn't reply. He didn't have to. How the man could say so much with just one look was beyond her, but it was obvious he knew way too much about her needs.

Lucas let his gaze travel over her body, taking his time as he studied every aspect of her. "You dress conservatively, but you know how to accentuate your strongest features. While you don't seek to hide the fact that you're very beautiful, your dress slacks, your simple silk blouse, and the understated jewelry prove that you wish to appear professional, not sexy. I assume that's something you—as a woman in a male-dominated world—have to be attuned to. You're every bit as intelligent as your male contemporaries and you are determined to be seen as such."

She shrugged, still struggling to recover from the needs he'd uncovered with just a few words and heated looks. "You've just described pretty much every woman in my profession."

"Are you daring me to dig deeper, Cait?"

She shivered at the dark tone in his voice that felt almost possessive.

She couldn't play this game anymore. Couldn't risk having him expose something she didn't want to acknowledge, especially to him. "Why are you at this pub?"

"You know why."

"Say it anyway."

"I want to buy it."

Chapter Two

Lucas would probably pay for showing his hand to the owner's granddaughter, but there was something about Caitlyn Wallace that knocked him off-kilter. He didn't like it. Found himself almost resenting her for it.

When she'd accepted his invitation for a drink, he knew she was hoping to get him to reveal his secrets. Not that he had any.

He'd made his intentions perfectly clear to her uncles and her mom. Lucas had known his first offer would be rejected. It was lowball, an insult probably, but he'd wanted to meet the owners, size them up. He didn't go into any business deal without knowing all the facts. He had a filing cabinet drawer full of everything anyone would ever want to know about Patrick Collins, his late wife, Sunday, and their large brood of children and grandchildren.

He had pictures of all of them, including their waitress, Ailis, and Caitlyn.

It was *her* picture he'd studied the most. He hadn't lied about her beauty. She took after her mother, with her long dark hair and striking pale blue eyes. They were the first things anyone who looked at her would see. And for any red-blooded heterosexual male, he didn't doubt they were more powerful than a siren's song, luring sailors to their death on the rocks.

Seeing her tonight in person and being taken in by those crystal eyes revealed just how potent they truly were. And it wasn't simply because of the color. It was the emotions reflected there that had ensnared him.

So far he'd seen them flash with anger toward her ex, wariness toward him and genuine affection for her uncle and cousin.

But more than that, he'd seen the one thing that could destroy all his well-laid plans.

Caitlyn was a submissive.

And he wanted her. Badly.

Lucas was accustomed to getting what he set his mind on, but Caitlyn's loyalty to her family would not be shaken, which currently put him in enemy camp.

Her next words solidified that. "You'll never get this pub."

"Never is a very dangerous word, Caitlyn. One that shouldn't be tossed around lightly."

"That doesn't apply in this situation. It's merely a statement of fact."

Lucas knew when to push and when to retreat. No war was ever won by a single march forward. In order to win, he needed to stage a series of battles, plot his advancement and accept that with every victory, there was bound to be a loss or two. The only thing that truly mattered to him was who was still standing at the end.

Four steps forward, three steps back still left him ahead at the end of the day.

"I don't want to be your enemy, Caitlyn."

"Then give up your quest."

The words "give up" weren't in his vocabulary, weren't in his genetic makeup, but she didn't need to know that. Yet.

"Fine."

Caitlyn narrowed her eyes in instant suspicion. "Fine?"

"Fine. I'll give up my quest—for now—on one condition."

He should have chosen his words more carefully. Lawyers always listen for the loophole. "For now?"

He chuckled. "Wouldn't you rather hear about the condition?"

"No."

He leaned forward and grasped her hand. Though she tried to tug it away from him, tried to hide the slight tremor in it, he didn't allow her retreat. He squeezed it gently, and then tightened his hold.

As he expected, her breathing hitched and her face flushed an even darker shade of red. Her initial blush had sent far too much blood south of the border, his cock stiffening as he slowly began to realize what she desperately tried to hide.

Caitlyn licked her lips. She was aroused, responding to his unyielding control.

"I want you to go out to dinner with me tomorrow night."

"That's the condition?"

He shook his head. "I'm attracted to you, Caitlyn. As you can imagine, that makes things," he paused, searching for the right word, "difficult for me, given my present desires."

"The pub."

He nodded. "I never mix business with pleasure."

"Never is a very dangerous word." Her tone, as she repeated his exact words back to him, revealed she was very pleased with herself.

"You're simply proving my point. I'm about to break that rule."

Caitlyn tried to draw her hand out of his grip once more, the action futile as he refused to relinquish it. Her eyes narrowed, no longer hazy with arousal. Now they flashed with anger. "I think you should lay out the terms of this condition as quickly as possible, because right now, I'm jumping to some terrible conclusions that make you look like the world's biggest prick. I'm about two seconds away from throwing the rest of this Guinness in your face and letting my uncles and cousins beat you to a pulp."

His jaw clenched when he realized how all of this sounded. He was handling this like a ham-fisted novice. The damn woman had knocked him for a loop. "You misunderstand me. I'm not saying I'll abandon my plan to buy this pub in exchange for sexual favors."

"Very wise of you."

"One date, Caitlyn. I would like to go out with you on one date. We won't discuss business at all."

She still didn't trust his motives. "And at the end of the night?"

"We'll decide if we want a second date."

"What happens if we want a third, and a fourth date after that?"

He sighed. "At some point, I hope you'll allow me to outline my plans for this pub, let me explain why selling it to me won't be the equivalent to making a deal with the devil."

Her face was resolute when she said once again, "We won't sell to you."

"So you keep saying." Lucas felt his attraction to her growing with each word she spoke. Her spine was straight, her shoulders stiff, her face imperious. Her determination to win only made her lovelier. And him more resolved.

In the end, he hoped to have the pub. *And* Caitlyn.

"Because it's true."

"What you haven't rejected yet is my invitation to a date."

She bit her lower lip briefly, drawing his attention to her mouth. He considered kissing her. It would take very little effort on his part to tug on the hand he held, to draw her closer. Part of him was tempted to try it simply to see exactly how many men in this pub would leap to her defense. He suspected half a dozen at least.

"I wouldn't suggest it," Caitlyn said, leaning nearer. She had no idea how tempting she was.

"Suggest what?"

"Kissing me. You're public enemy number one in here right now."

He fucking wanted her. His cock was stiff as a pike. "Say yes to my offer."

She still hesitated.

Just as he thought. Her loyalty to her family ran deep. Very deep.

However, there was something else buried next to devotion. Something fighting just as hard to make its way to the surface.

He brushed his thumb along the top of the hand he still held. She hadn't pulled away after her warning, which meant he only needed to lean forward the tiniest bit. Their lips were inches apart. "Say yes, Cait," he whispered, perfectly aware of the demand lacing his tone.

"Yes." Her response was more breath than sound, but it was enough for him to hear.

And it came a mere millisecond before three burly Irishmen surrounded their table.

"Everything okay over here, Caitlyn?" her uncle Tris asked.

She tried to tug her hand from his grip, but Lucas refused to relent, refused to show the slightest inkling of fear or weakness. The Collins men were clearly used to their intimidation techniques working. However, they'd never met a Whiting. Lucas's father had written the manual on bullying.

"Everything is fine," Lucas said. "Caitlyn just agreed to go out with me tomorrow."

"She did no such thing," Ewan insisted. All three men turned their attention to Caitlyn. Lucas wasn't sure what reaction he expected from her, but it wasn't what she did.

She stood, no longer bothering to try to reclaim her hand. Instead, she squeezed *his*. Hard. Really fucking hard.

As she did so, she faced down the other three men. "Actually, I did. Lucas and I are going out on a date."

"Lucas?" her cousin Colm—or possibly Padraig—said. Tristan had identical twin sons, so it was anyone's guess which one this was. Lucas assumed it was Colm, because he looked the lawyer type and he'd walked in with Caitlyn earlier.

"We're not having this conversation right here in front of the entire pub," she said through gritted teeth. "I'm an adult and perfectly capable of making my own decisions, as you know."

Mr. Collins stepped next to Tris. "Am I missing something fun?"

Lucas grinned at the old man's jest, but the other four people at the table visibly stiffened.

"No, Pop," Tris said quickly. "Not at all."

Despite his advanced age, Patrick Collins appeared to be no one's fool. He studied the hard expressions on his sons' and grandson's faces, then turned his attention to him and Caitlyn, his sharp gaze taking in the fact they were still holding hands.

"Caitie-bug. Who's your friend?"

Lucas fought to keep his face impassive, trying to hide his surprise. Patrick Collins didn't know who he was? This was an unexpected development.

"This is Lucas," Caitlyn said, purposely not saying his last name.

Lucas stood and reached out with his free hand. "Nice to meet you, Mr. Collins."

"You too, son. You and my granddaughter here on a date?"

Lucas could feel himself being sized up by Patrick, not as the man who wanted to buy his pub, but as the man who wanted to date his "Caitie-bug."

Lucas figured he'd probably be found more worthy to take the pub—and that was as likely as ice sculptures in hell.

For now, however, he was focusing on the undercurrents pulsing around the table. Why hadn't Patrick been told about his offer to buy the pub?

"No, sir," Lucas said. "We were just having a quick drink. She and I are going out tomorrow."

While the other men still didn't seem to agree with that assertion, they held their tongues.

"Oh, that's wonderful. Been trying to get our Caitie to go out for months and have some fun. Are you a lawyer too, Lucas?"

Lucas shook his head, enjoying the way Tristan's jaw clenched tightly. He was just enough of a bastard to get a kick out of holding the upper hand. He had these men over a barrel, and all of them knew it. "I'm in real estate."

"Really? Do you—"

"Look at that, Pop," Ewan said, pointing to the TV screen. "The Caps just scored."

Patrick's eyes lit up. "Hot damn." He rubbed his hands together and turned back toward the bar. "I have twenty dollars riding on this game."

The older man returned to the bar and his cronies, all of them enjoying the replay and declaring there was no way the Caps weren't capturing the Stanley Cup this year.

"Shit," Colm muttered, his eyes also glued to the TV.

"You bet against Pop Pop? Wait. You bet against the Caps?" Caitlyn asked in disbelief. "Who are they playing?"

"Pittsburgh," Colm mumbled, as if he was embarrassed to say it too loud.

"Pittsburgh?! We fucking hate Pittsburgh," Caitlyn cried.

"Language," Patrick called out to his granddaughter from across the room.

"Better not let your dad hear you say that," Ewan warned, though it was obvious he approved of his niece's disdain. "He's never given up his love of the dark side, though God knows we've all tried to beat that loyalty out of him."

Lucas hoped the term "beat" was figurative. He'd heard this Irish clan was bloodthirsty when it came to sports, but brawling over them seemed extreme.

"Your father roots for Pittsburgh?" Lucas asked.

Caitlyn nodded. "Born and raised there."

Colm ran his hand through his hair in frustration. "Caps goalie is on injured reserve. Everybody knows they've got nothing on the bench." If Colm had felt any need to defend his cousin's honor, it appeared the hockey game wiped it away as he returned to his stool at the bar, cursing the TV, the lost twenty, and the Penguins, not exactly in that order.

"Are we finished now?" Caitlyn asked her uncles.

"We'll talk later," Tris said, returning to the bar. Ewan gave her a worried look, but didn't say anything more before heading back to the restaurant side.

Lucas imagined she would be in for quite an earful from her uncles after he left.

"Listen, Lucas, I don't think—"

She planned to back out. It wasn't going to work.

"I'll pick you up tomorrow at seven."

"No, really—"

"Why didn't anyone tell Mr. Collins about my offer?"

She grimaced. "We will. If it becomes necessary."

"Are you afraid he'll accept it?"

Caitlyn laughed. "You should probably do a little more research, because it's clear you don't know the first thing about any of us."

Her words taunted him in a way she didn't intend. Regardless, he reacted, ready to set her straight.

"I know a lot more about you than you're going to be comfortable with, Cait. Wear a dress tomorrow. And no panties."

Her cheeks pinkened, but not with anger, though that was certainly what she wanted him to believe. "You pompous son of a—"

He gripped her waist with one hand, the other tipping her face up, forcing her to look him straight in the eye. "We're not going to dance around the obvious. And I'm not going to let you deny who you are when you're with me. Dress. No panties. That is the last time I will ever repeat my wishes to you. Do you understand?"

Caitlyn blinked several times and for a moment, he wasn't sure she was breathing.

When she finally did respond, he was the one who had all the wind knocked out of his system.

"Yes, sir."

Chapter Three

Caitlyn tugged down the hem of her dress and checked herself once more in the mirror. The black sheath came to mid-thigh, so there was no way anyone would know she was panty-less. Even so, *she* knew.

She glanced at the bed, where she'd tossed her panties. She had pulled them on three times since getting dressed. And every time, she'd slipped them off again. The fact that she was following Lucas's directive was driving her crazy. They'd only just met. Why on earth would she feel this unyielding need to obey him? He was nothing to her.

"Shit," she mumbled. This was not a man she should be going out with, let alone indulging in D/s play. She didn't know Lucas Whiting from Adam, and she sure as hell didn't trust him.

She reached for her panties once again. And then she stuffed them in the drawer, putting them out of sight.

Fuck me.

This was bad. Very bad.

She'd done her Google search on Lucas Whiting about three minutes after he'd left last night. And while she had found out quite a bit, she still had a million and twelve questions about him. Actually, all she'd really discovered, apart from his net worth and vast property dealings, was surface-y stuff. Details that told her nothing about the man he was underneath the skin. The only personal information she'd acquired was that he was thirty-nine years old and he hadn't lied about his marital status...or lack thereof.

A wolf whistle sounded from the doorway, and she turned to see Ailis grinning at her.

"You look hot. You sure you want to go that route?"

Caitlyn shook her head. "If I was smart, I'd pin my hair up in a bun, wipe off all the makeup, and dress like a nun."

"Given the way Lucas was looking at you last night, I'm pretty sure none of that would drive him away. It doesn't matter now, anyway. We're running out of time. I've been sent to fetch you for your intervention."

Caitlyn rolled her eyes. "Seriously?"

Interventions were not uncommon in her family. If the Collins cousins felt one of their own was making a mistake, they formed a united front to confront the offender head-on. Hell, Caitlyn had just organized an intervention for Colm several months earlier when the jackass had decided he looked good with a goatee. They'd nipped that in the bud quickly and convinced him to shave.

Ailis gave her a guilty one-shoulder shrug. "Sorry. You sort of sealed your fate when you held hands with the man trying to steal the pub from us."

"He's not stealing it. He made an offer to buy— legitimately—and we said no. Game over."

"You don't really think that's the end of it, do you? He's Lucas *Whiting*." Ailis stressed his last name, solidifying even more why Caitlyn should be wearing the biggest granny panties she could find.

Rather than allowing her to respond, Ailis turned and headed toward the living room. Caitlyn took a deep breath and followed. She'd escaped to her office at the crack of dawn this morning in an attempt to dodge this confrontation, and she had only returned home an hour earlier, hopping in the shower and then hiding in her bedroom while waging the great panty debate.

Glancing around the crowded living room, she groaned. "Oh my God. It's one flipping date."

The room was packed with too many relatives. In addition to Ailis, there were the twins, Padraig and Colm, as well as Sunnie, Yvonne, Finn, and Caitlyn's brother Lochlan. And while most of them lived in the dorm, it was rare for all of them to be home at the same time.

Lochlan stood and gestured for her to take his seat. "We know that, but Lucas Whiting isn't the kind of man you want dating your sister."

She sank down on the couch next to Finn, who said, "We've been digging around for information on the guy ever since he made his offer to buy the pub. Dad has heard plenty of rumors over the years about the Whitings." Finn's dad, Aaron, was married to her aunt Riley. He was also a Baltimore cop, so it stood to reason that Uncle Aaron would know quite a bit about the Whiting family.

"What sort of rumors?" Caitlyn asked, realizing she'd be smart to arm herself with more information. Maybe some of the finer details would help her resist this sexual pull she felt toward Lucas.

"God, where should we start?" Yvonne said. "For one thing, his brother overdosed on heroin a year ago."

Well, that didn't help. Caitlyn shrugged. "So we're assuming the whole family are addicts now?"

Yvonne shook her head. "No, of course not. That's just one of the things we know for sure. Along with the fact his parents are alive, though divorced, and Lucas plays a big role in the family businesses. That stuff is all truth. The rest..."

"Is just conjecture," Colm continued. "But there are enough stories flying around that we think you should proceed with caution."

"Okay. Lay it on me," Caitlyn said, not certain why she suddenly felt the need to defend Lucas to her cousins.

Lochlan started the list. "He employs cutthroat, take-no-prisoners business tactics. I know some people who've gone head-to-head with Lucas Whiting. Apparently he's got the mayor, half of the city council, not to mention a couple of senators in his back pocket. He makes healthy donations to political campaigns...with the expectation that his generosity will be repaid in favors."

Sunnie leaned forward in her chair. "Mom said there have been rumors flying around Baltimore for years that the Whitings are connected to the mob."

"Aunt Riley probably heard that from Bubbles," Caitlyn said. "She thinks everyone works for the mob."

Sunnie grinned and didn't disagree.

"I started asking around about him at the pub after his last visit. No one can recall the guy ever dating anyone for any amount of time. He attends plenty of social events with dates, but he's never been seen with the same woman more than once. Don't you think that's kind of weird?" Padraig worked beside his dad, Tris, tending bar in the pub. As such, he knew more than he probably cared to know about Baltimore's social scene.

"So the guy's a commitment-phobe." Caitlyn didn't think that was much of an argument. Actually, none of their attempts had been very convincing.

"Or…after every date, he takes the woman home and tosses her in a dungeon as part of some secret harem. Or he's killing them and chopping them up as part of some sick experiment," Sunnie added with wide eyes.

"You gotta lay off the horror flicks, Sun," Padraig teased. Sunnie was far too enamored of that movie genre and they all knew it. She was only a couple more twisted comments away from an intervention of her own.

Caitlyn really—really—wanted to laugh at that exchange, but she'd fixated on the word dungeon a little too hard.

She cleared her throat and shook it off. "I'm not planning to do more than go out to dinner with him, figure out what his plans are in regards to the pub and then come home to fill you all in. The fact that he doesn't date a woman more than once should set your mind at ease."

"So you're just going out with him to spy?" Ailis asked.

"Why else?" Caitlyn asked.

Ailis shrugged. "I don't know. I thought you both looked pretty into each other last night."

Caitlyn didn't know how to reply. Mainly because she *had* been attracted to Lucas. Like off-the-charts attracted. She'd been hoping perhaps some of that had worn off and tonight she'd be better able to deal with him. Of course, given the fact she wasn't wearing panties, it was probably a safe bet that hadn't happened.

The intervention was cut short by a knock on the door. No one moved to answer it.

"I don't suppose I can convince you guys to scatter, so it doesn't look like he's walking into the Spanish Inquisition."

Lochlan crossed his arms. "Go open the door, Caitlyn. We're not budging."

She blew out an exasperated breath. "You're all insane." She rose and opened the door. And knew in an instant it wasn't her family who was crazy.

It was her.

Lucas wore black dress pants and a deep blue designer button-down shirt that looked imported and probably cost more than her monthly car payment. His thick dark hair was neatly combed—which made her fingers itch to mess it up—and he appeared to have trimmed his beard.

His gaze drifted down as he took in her dress, clearly approving. The corners of his mouth tipped up in a barely there smile that set her heart racing. He oozed sex appeal, confidence, power, and wealth.

She was in over her head.

"You look beautiful, Caitlyn."

A male throat cleared behind her, and she closed her eyes briefly. "I'm sorry about this," she muttered as she took a step back to let him get a clear view of the crowded living room. "This is my family."

Lucas grinned, seemingly unperturbed by their audience. "Nice to meet you," he said to the room in general.

Lochlan walked over. "I'm Caitlyn's brother."

"Lochlan. Yes, I know."

Caitlyn wished Lucas had kept that tidbit to himself. Her brother's expression darkened. He clearly didn't appreciate the idea that Lucas had done his homework on their family. It proved that the threat they were all feeling was very real.

She wasn't about to launch into any more introductions. God only knew what else Lucas would reveal. Caitlyn didn't relish the thought of having to bail one of her cousins or her brother out of jail for assault. "Should we go?" She reached for the clutch she'd put on a side table near the door.

"Of course." Lucas placed his hand at the base of her back possessively, intent on guiding her out. Lochlan didn't miss the touch, or the challenge behind it, and his scowl grew more pronounced.

"Have a good night," Lucas said to her brother smoothly, adding fuel to the fire. Caitlyn had the strong desire to throat punch her date. And then her brother.

Fucking men.

Fucking testosterone.

She refused to be the prize in a pissing match.

Of course, simply walking out of the apartment didn't get her out of the lion's den. Caitlyn felt Uncle Tris's eyes follow her as she and Lucas left the pub together. Mercifully, he didn't stop them or try to engage in conversation. Chances were good he knew about the intervention upstairs and figured she'd already been told everything she needed to know.

Sadly, her cousins' rumors and warnings had started to take root. She clutched her purse more tightly, hoping to hide her shaking hands as Lucas opened the passenger door to his Jaguar for her. She climbed in and closed her eyes as he shut the door and walked to the driver's side.

What was she doing here?

Once Lucas was behind the wheel, he turned to look at her. "Are you okay?"

She nodded once, then shook her head. "No."

"Been doing research on me?"

The man was too clever, but she didn't bother to lie. "Yes, I have."

He didn't start the car. Instead, he held her gaze. "Let's have it. What did you find out?"

Caitlyn didn't hold back. Part of her hoped he'd confess everything her cousins told her was true. Maybe then she'd find the strength to get out of this car and walk away.

"Mob connections?"

He grinned. "Do you think I'd admit that if it were true?"

She narrowed her eyes, waiting for a better answer.

"No. My family doesn't work with mobsters. We operate within the boundaries of the law. Most of the time."

He'd added the last as a joke, but Caitlyn suspected there was a vein of truth to it.

"Sounds like it's easy to be on the up-and-up when you're able to convince the mayor to do your bidding."

"My family has been very generous to his campaign."

"That's not an answer."

"You didn't ask a question."

Asshole.

"Do you use your connections to the mayor and city council to your advantage? Are you able to convince those people to do your bidding in order to get your way?"

He nodded. "Absolutely."

"Could you use your sway with them to find a way to force my family to sell you the pub?"

Lucas hesitated, which was answer enough in her mind. Even so, she let the question stand, interested in hearing his reply. If he lied to her, she was getting out of this car and going back inside.

"I could," he admitted.

"Will you?"

"We agreed we weren't going to talk about business tonight."

"That's not an answer." She wasn't going to back down.

Unfortunately, Lucas wasn't the type of man who was easily cowed. "You and I both know the answer to that question, Caitlyn."

She glanced out the passenger window at the pub. "You're an asshole," she muttered. She needed to get out of this car. The man had just admitted he'd stop at nothing to take the pub away from her family. Yet she still didn't reach for the door handle.

"You aren't the first to inform me of that. And I doubt you'll be the last. I've been completely honest with you. I'm not hiding anything."

"That doesn't make me feel any better."

"Me, either. This would all be a hell of a lot easier if I weren't so intrigued by you. You're intelligent, beautiful and funny, and I really want to take you out tonight. But I won't blame you if you get out of the car."

She hesitated. Intrigued was an excellent word. And the main thing that had her acting so selfishly.

"Tell you what. You can order the most expensive thing on the menu just to run up the tab. That way you'll be able to justify going out with such a bastard."

She laughed, wishing for the millionth time that she weren't so attracted to him. Her life would be so much simpler if the guy repulsed her.

"A free meal is pretty tempting. Where are we going?"

"The Carleson."

Her eyes widened. "Wow. I've always wanted to go there, but reservations are booked out for months. I've heard the food is incredible."

He smiled. "So we're doing the date?"

She nodded. "Yeah. We're doing it."

"Good." Lucas started the car, weaving them through the weekend traffic with skill as they made small talk about the weather, where they went to school, and their favorite Baltimore bars.

When they pulled up in front of the restaurant, Lucas handed the keys to the valet, and then took her hand as they entered.

The maître d' led them to what he called the wine library. Caitlyn was surprised to discover there was only one table in the large room. It was tucked in an intimate corner and surrounded on two sides by massive shelves containing hundreds of bottles of wine.

Their table was round and covered with a long white cloth. A single candlestick served as the simple yet elegant centerpiece. The lighting in the room was dim, and soft music played. It was breathtakingly romantic.

The maître d' pushed in her chair for her as Lucas claimed the other. Rather than sitting across from each other, the seats were placed side-by-side, close enough that Lucas's knee brushed hers as he sat.

The maître d' gestured to the bottle of wine already chilling on the table. "Shall I pour?"

Lucas nodded, and they sat quietly as the man filled their glasses. Then he promised to send the waiter in to check on them.

When they were alone, she looked around once more. "You reserved the entire room?"

"I wanted to ensure we had privacy."

"Why?"

Lucas chuckled. "Don't look at me as if I'm about to make you my main course. People tend to gawk when they figure out who I am. I don't enjoy being under a microscope when I'm out on a date."

"Ah. Well, that sort of explains one of the other rumors flying around about you."

Lucas tilted his head curiously. "What rumor?"

"Your personal life seems to be devoid of long-term relationships. No one ever sees you out with a girlfriend. Probably because you hide them in the cozy corners of exclusive restaurants. Is this your usual spot when you're trying to impress a woman?"

"No. It's not."

Lucas reached over and took her hand in his. She wasn't used to a man holding her hand. She wished it didn't feel so good.

"If you want to know more about my past relationships, Caitlyn, all you have to do is ask."

"Fine. What was your longest relationship?"

"Three months."

Caitlyn choked on the sip of wine she'd just taken. "Three months?"

"I was in Paris for five weeks of that, so I'll let you decide if those weeks should be included in the tally."

She bit her lower lip, debating whether she should ask her next question. She didn't want to seem rude.

Lucas noticed. "You clearly want to know more. Ask."

"Is there a reason why you avoid committed relationships?"

"I don't purposely keep my affairs short. In truth, I'm incredibly busy. I work very long hours and I travel quite a lot. Because of that, it's difficult to start a relationship. I may go out with a woman whose company I enjoy, but because of work commitments, it could be a week or a month before I'm able to see her again. I don't seem able to make it over the hump between casual dating and long-term relationship."

"Oh." Caitlyn thought that sounded like a pretty lonely way to live, but she kept that thought to herself.

"Can I ask you a question?"

She nodded.

"How long were you with Sammy?"

Caitlyn crinkled her nose, embarrassed to admit the truth. "Three years."

"That's a long time. Especially considering you rejected his marriage proposal. Why did you stay with him if you didn't want to marry him?"

That was definitely something she was too embarrassed to say, so she just shrugged.

"I'm going to go out on a limb and guess that the sex was good. At least, he seemed to think so."

She laughed despite herself. "I realize that makes me sound shallow as hell, but I had two longish relationships prior to Sammy and the sex was strictly vanilla. It bored me to tears. At least with him it was..." She paused, wishing she could erase everything she'd just revealed.

"It was?" he prodded.

"Better," she supplied, suddenly mortified by what she'd revealed. Had she seriously just bitched about vanilla sex?

"Did you engage in D/s play with Sammy?"

She felt her cheeks heat. She hated Lucas's ability to make her blush. She was usually impossible to fluster. "I...don't think...you and I should talk about—"

"It's a simple question, Cait. Yes or no?"

Her body responded to his deep voice, and she noticed he shortened her name anytime he took on that tone that made her want to kneel in front of him.

"Sort of."

Lucas frowned. "Sort of?"

"Sammy was more open-minded about my desires than my previous boyfriends. He was willing to experiment with me. To try some of the things I wanted."

"I see."

She was afraid he saw all too well. Probably because she was drawing him a freaking road map. "I can't believe I told you all that. We just met."

"I'm glad you told me."

She tugged her hand free of his and took another sip of wine, her mind frantically racing on some different topic of conversation. They'd gotten way too personal, too fast.

"This wine is incredible."

"I wasn't sure if you liked red. The blanc seemed like a safer choice. For future reference, where do you stand on reds?"

Caitlyn grinned mischievously, grateful to guide them back to the cat-and-mouse game. It was easier for her to maneuver through. "Future reference? That sure of yourself, are you?"

He didn't respond. Instead, he pressed for the answer. "A simple love it or hate it will do."

"I love all reds. Except merlot."

"So noted."

"Since you seem to know every single detail about my family, how about you tell me a little bit about yours. You work with your dad, right?"

Lucas nodded. "I joined Whiting Properties after earning an MBA from Harvard. I'm COO to my father's CEO title."

She'd read that fact in his bio on the company's website. "You and your dad must be close."

Padraig and Tris worked together at the bar, and the two of them were thick as thieves. Aunt Lane joked that she thought they actually shared a hive mind. Padraig would start a story and Tris would finish it. Or Tris would simply jerk his head toward the liquor shelf and somehow Padraig knew exactly which bottle he needed.

"If you're referring to proximity, then yes, my dad and I are close. His office is next door to mine."

His short tone took her aback. "I didn't mean physical distance."

"I know. My father isn't exactly an easy man to get close to. He's…" Lucas paused and Caitlyn sensed he was trying to find the words. "He's a perfectionist, and he expects nothing less than that in everyone who works for him. He's driven and detail-oriented. If you've done a good job, he won't say anything to you. That's his version of a compliment. If you've displeased him, you'll know it, because where he lacks kind words, he has an endless supply of criticism. Failure isn't tolerated. Ever."

"Jesus. He sounds like a mean son of a bitch."

Lucas chuckled. "He is. Very much so."

"Is that why your mother left?" Caitlyn winced.

Wow. Nosy much?

He must have noticed her unease. "I don't mind the questions. I know exactly how much information is floating around about the Whitings online. I already admitted I've done my research on your family as well. My mother was an heiress, wealthy in her own right before she married my father. They're equals when it comes to their love of money and power. When they met, no doubt they saw a way to double that wealth. Unfortunately, greed wasn't a strong enough reason to stay together in the end. I once saw a really old movie with Michael Douglas called *War of the Roses*. Have you ever seen it?"

Caitlyn shook her head.

"You should look it up sometime. It fits my parents to a tee."

"How old were you when they divorced?"

"Twelve. Which in my mind was eleven years too late."

"Do you see your mom often?"

"We have a standing lunch date at her country club once a month, where she apprises me of business matters concerning her inheritance...and mine. Typically the meal lasts anywhere from two to three hours, which is long enough for both of us."

Caitlyn spoke to her mom nearly every single day. Not because she had to, but because she wanted to. And she talked to her dad almost as much. They were interested in her day-to-day life and always there to offer advice or a shoulder to cry on if she needed it. Once again, she was struck by how different their lives were. How lonely his must be.

"I can't imagine it was easy for you growing up in a home like that. With people like that."

Lucas had been looking at her very directly for most of their conversation, but now his gaze dropped to his wineglass. He toyed with the stem. "I handled it better than most."

"I guess so. Considering you're still willing to work with your father."

"The business is half mine. My father and I have worked very hard to make it prosperous and successful. We have similar goals and...for lack of a better word...mindsets. As such, it's not difficult working with him. However, others don't feel the same. We've lost more than our fair share of business admins."

"Because of your dad? Or you too?" she asked with a grin.

"I can see by your smile you know the answer to that question perfectly well. As you said in the car, I'm a bastard by my own right."

"I said asshole. Bastard was your word."

Lucas chuckled.

"And where did your brother figure into all of this?"

The second the question came out, Caitlyn wished she could pull it back in. She'd always been far too inquisitive, wearing her parents out with queries about everything under the sun when she was growing up. Her dad assured her that her tenaciousness and constant probing for answers was one of the reasons she was a good lawyer. However, in this case, she'd gone too far. Left the realm of curious and entered the world of prying, nosy bitch.

"Please forget I asked that. It was horribly rude of me to—"

"No," Lucas interrupted her. "You've done your homework well. I don't mind answering. My brother, Toby..." Lucas paused. "Well, he took everything our father said to heart."

Caitlyn reached out, grasping his hand. "I heard that he passed away. I shouldn't have brought it up. I'm very sorry."

He squeezed her hand and gave her a sad smile. "The coroner said it was a drug overdose."

There was something in his tone that told her he didn't agree with that assessment.

"It wasn't?"

Her suspicions were confirmed when he very quietly added, "I know it was suicide."

Caitlyn swallowed heavily, searching his face for some trace of the emotion she heard in his voice. Strangely, it was missing. While he'd shared a very painful secret with her, he somehow still managed to hold himself aloof, stoic.

As such, she didn't have a clue how to respond. She would be devastated to lose Lochlan or one of her cousins to suicide. She could only imagine how often Lucas played over events or conversations, wondering if there was something he could have done to save his brother. God knew that was what she would do. Finally, she repeated, "I'm so sorry."

"You're wasting your degree."

Caitlyn frowned. "What do you mean?"

"You were made for criminal courts. You've managed to get me to confess things I've never told anyone."

"Why *did* you tell me all that?"

He ran his thumb along the top of her hand. "You asked."

Did that mean no one had ever bothered to get to know him on a personal level? That idea saddened her, though she could understand why it was true. Lucas's brooding face and no-nonsense way of speaking didn't exactly invite someone to seek confidences.

They held hands for a few moments longer, only letting go when the waiter returned with a rich-looking lobster soup. Once the bowls were set in front of them, he topped up their wineglasses and left again.

She glanced at the soup curiously, considering she hadn't even seen a menu yet.

"I took the liberty of placing our order when I made the reservation. Pace yourself. There are five more courses coming."

Her eyes widened. "Five?"

Lucas grinned. "That was the most expensive thing on the menu."

She lifted the spoon and took a taste of the soup. She closed her eyes and groaned at the sheer delicious decadence of it. "Oh my God."

When she lifted her eyelids, she realized Lucas wasn't eating. Instead, he was watching her—hungrily. Clearly what was in the bowl wasn't going to sate his desires.

"Lucas," she whispered. She was two seconds away from suggesting they skip straight to dessert.

She shut the thought down. She wasn't sleeping with him. She couldn't.

Could she?

"Did you obey my command?"

Oh fuck.

"I can't do this with you."

Lucas's eyes narrowed, his gaze going dark. That look should have terrified her. Instead, she was more aroused than she'd ever been in her life. "Answer my question, Cait."

Again with the nickname. She'd been called Cait a million times in her life by pretty much everyone she knew. Yet somehow, when he used that tone, it took on a completely different feeling, different meaning to her.

"I can't." Caitlyn lowered her eyes, humiliated by the way her voice broke. This was too complicated for her.

He let her off the hook. "When did you first realize you were submissive?"

She clasped her hands together in her lap, trying to resist this. Sadly, she didn't want to. While she had tried to explain her desires to Sammy, it was obvious he'd never truly understood them, never gotten what made her tick.

There was something about Lucas that made her want to reveal all her secrets. Probably because there wasn't a doubt in her mind he was the man she'd been looking for her entire life.

No.

Not man.

Dom.

While she disagreed with pretty much everything he stood for—greed and power and squeezing out the little guy—none of those things made it any easier for her to resist him. Because she desperately wanted what he could offer her in the bedroom.

"I guess I—"

"Look at me when you answer, Cait."

Her gaze returned to his face. It was soft and hard at the same time, which left her even more confused.

"High school. I dated a boy for several months my junior year. He was a year older, controlling, jealous. He wasn't acting that way because he was a Dom. The truth is he was a jerk, but I felt aroused by…weird things."

"Like what?"

"We got into a fight once. He saw me talking to some guy in the cafeteria. He went berserk, yelling at me. I was fed up with him so I turned around, started to walk away. He grabbed my arm and twisted me back to face him. He pushed me against the wall of the school and kissed me hard. Told me I belonged to him."

"And while you didn't like the guy, you liked what he was saying. Liked the rough edge, the control."

She nodded. "My parents…"

Lucas leaned closer. "Your mother is a sub."

"Yes. I've never witnessed anything outright between them, but I just know. It was my mom who pulled me aside when things with that first boyfriend got out of hand. She said some of my feelings weren't wrong, but *he* was."

"Smart lady."

"The problem is *all* the men I've dated in my life have been the wrong ones. The first two guys couldn't wrap their heads around what I wanted from them. They thought I was asking for them to abuse me. They were nice guys who just didn't get it. And while Sammy was game, he wasn't a natural Dom. It always felt like I was in control, telling him what to do."

"Topping from the bottom."

Caitlyn sighed.

"Why do you say you can't do this with me? Is it because of the pub? Your family?"

"Partly."

He raised one eyebrow, telling her without words he expected her to tell him the whole truth.

"The other part of me is terrified because of that whole 'be careful what you wish for' adage. I know you can give me what I want. But…"

"You think I'm the wrong man too."

"Will you give up on the pub?"

"No."

She hated and respected his complete honesty.

"Cait, I would never force myself on an unwilling woman."

"I didn't insinuate—"

"I want you to lift the hem of your dress and part your legs."

The tablecloth was long, and they were completely alone in the room. The placement of the table was perfect because no one could see them even if they walked in. However, the waiter could come back at any moment, and if he approached the table, he would see what they were doing.

She'd never indulged in this sort of play in public. She and Sammy limited their sexual experimentation to their apartment.

"Pick a safe word." He acted as if the decision had already been made.

"I told you—"

"Blue. Your safe word is blue. Say that, and I'll look into those soul-stealing eyes of yours and deny you nothing."

Caitlyn struggled to get air into her lungs. She was light-headed, her vision going fuzzy. If she didn't remember how to breathe soon, she'd pass out.

"The decision is yours, Cait. I've made the request. If you do as I ask, I want you to understand you're saying yes not only to me touching you here in the restaurant, but to me taking you home tonight. To me claiming control of your body, your pleasure, your pain, your orgasms...even your mind."

"And if I don't want that?"

"Keep your legs closed and we'll simply continue to enjoy each other's company."

"And at the end of the night?"

"I'll take you home and kiss you good night."

He was offering her everything she'd always wanted sexually and feared she'd never find. Lucas told her last night that everyone had a bottom line. He'd found hers in just twenty-four hours. If she opened her legs, she would have the opportunity to experience a night in the arms of a true Dom.

What if she never got this chance again? She was nearly thirty-three and she'd never met a man like Lucas.

Regardless, she needed a safety net.

"If I go home with you..." her words came out haltingly, hesitantly.

"Yes?"

"It's just for tonight."

Lucas scowled. "What do you mean?"

"I don't want more than tonight. No more sex. No more dates. Nothing. We both return to opposite sides of the battle and this is over."

She could tell he wanted to argue, to refuse her request. If anyone asked her, Caitlyn would swear she didn't do one-night stands. To her, sex was an extension of emotion. She had to feel something for the men she went to bed with.

But she couldn't let herself feel anything for Lucas beyond desire. If she did, it would consume her, swallow her whole, leave her in ruin.

She tugged the skirt of her dress lower, pressing her knees together so tightly her thigh muscles burned.

Lucas's gaze dropped to her lap, and his frown grew more pronounced. "One night."

She'd never heard two words laced with such disdain, such anger, but Lucas had agreed to her condition.

"Say your safe word. Let me hear it."

"Blue," she whispered.

"Open your legs."

Caitlyn didn't even try to hide her trembling hands. The response had absolutely nothing to do with fear and apparently Lucas knew it. He'd given her the word, the way out.

That knowledge made it easier for her to let go, to stop trying to control her emotions, her panting breaths, her shaking hands.

She slid the hem of the skirt all the way to her waist and parted her legs. She didn't look down. Instead, her gaze was glued to Lucas's face, desperate to see his reaction when he realized she'd obeyed his command. That she'd left the panties at home.

Caitlyn had expected him to smile, to give some sign that he was pleased or even that he'd won, that he'd gotten his way. What she got was more potent, more dangerous, and for a split second, she considered saying her safe word.

Lucas's eyes rose to hers, and she knew in that instant, she was lost.

Lucas cupped her cheek with one hand and mouthed the word, "Mine."

Chapter Four

He was a fucking liar.

Lucas had promised Caitlyn one night, but that wasn't going to happen. There was no way he was going to let her walk away from him so easily. There was too much he wanted to do with her, and they weren't going to touch the tip of the iceberg tonight.

She was shaking, breathing heavily as her chest rose and fell rapidly. He could almost imagine he saw the pulse in her neck beating roughly from her pounding heart. She was afraid. Not of what he'd do, but of what he'd make her feel.

And feel she would.

The flat of his hand on her bare ass.

His fingers gripping her hair, pulling it until her scalp burned.

His cock fucking her pussy, her ass, her mouth.

His lips and teeth on her nipples. They were budded, poking through the thin material of her dress, daring him to take a bite.

There was no part of her he wouldn't claim.

Caitlyn wasn't the type of woman to give up control easily, though it was clear she desperately wanted to. If he hoped to ensnare her, to keep her, he would have to show her that she was wrong.

He was the perfect man for her in bed.

The only man for her.

Her pussy was trimmed, but he preferred it completely shaved. Perhaps he'd take care of that himself tonight.

He glanced across the room, at the reflection in the glass doors covering the shelves of wine. It gave him the perfect view of the door and the hallway, allowing him to see the waiter approaching before he entered the room.

Lucas hadn't merely called to make the reservation. He'd come in person earlier this afternoon in order to set everything up according to his wishes.

Caitlyn would experience trepidation about the possibility of someone walking in on them and that would fuel her excitement. Her nervousness. She didn't need to know that he was protecting her modesty. Like right now.

He tugged her dress back down and placed her napkin on her lap mere seconds before the waiter returned with the next course.

"Iberico chorizo," the waiter said as he placed the sausage in front of them. While it looked delicious, garnished with arugula, fresh tomatoes and rosemary, Lucas doubted he'd even taste it.

He was too focused on Caitlyn's submission. She was inexperienced, yet Caitlyn knew who she was, what she wanted in bed. She simply hadn't found the right man to give it to her.

God willing, he intended to be that man. He'd played with quite a few subs over the years, just as he'd had some fairly vanilla affairs. Lucas was dominant by nature and he enjoyed control in the bedroom, but he didn't need it. He didn't want a slave 24/7. For him, D/s games were not a lifestyle, nor would they ever be.

Caitlyn was too independent, too strong-willed and opinionated to give total control of her life to a man. But her body, her sexual pleasure…that was something else.

The waiter asked if everything was to their liking and then he left them alone again.

Caitlyn picked up her fork and took a bite of the chorizo.

"The waiter is no longer here, Cait."

She blinked a couple of times and then, slowly, she tugged the napkin off her lap, drew her dress back up and parted her legs.

Unable to resist, he reached down, running a single finger along her slit.

She gasped as he confirmed she was wet.

He flicked her clit, just once, enjoying the way her cheeks flushed even deeper.

"Pain or submission?"

She didn't blink at the question. "Both."

"Which is stronger?"

This time she did hesitate. "I…"

God. He saw her struggle to decide. She was beautiful. Perfect.

"It doesn't matter," he said, letting her off the hook. She'd told him exactly what he needed to know. She would submit to him, accept his commands. Just as she would respond to the pain. She'd never had a man take complete control of her, push her limits, force her out of her comfort zone.

Lucas intended to do all three. There was nothing sexier than a strong, intelligent woman's submission.

She'd told him he could only have one night. He fully intended to claim much more than that. He was no stranger to people telling him no. Just as he knew exactly how to change their minds.

The bottom line.

"Eat your chorizo, Cait."

She picked up her fork, stabbing a piece of the sausage and putting it into her mouth. He followed suit. The tension at the table was palpable. Thick.

Neither of them bothered to converse. Instead, he watched her as she waited for him to do something, wary as a young deer stalked by a mountain lion. She didn't know when he was going to pounce. Only that he was.

Once they finished their chorizo, he took another sip of wine. Caitlyn reached for her glass as well, but he grasped her wrist, stopping her. "You've had enough for tonight."

The corners of her lips tipped up in the perfect combination of grin and grimace. "I think more wine would make tonight a lot easier."

He returned her smile, though he suspected she viewed it as threat more than comfort. "I don't want tonight to be easy for you. You need to be challenged."

His words must have tweaked the part of her that still resisted this part of her genetic makeup. "And you think you're up to that task?"

Lucas reached out and took her nipple between his finger and thumb. He pinched it roughly. "Don't taunt me or play the brat, Cait. I'm not like the other fools you've taken to your bed. You won't goad me into doing your bidding."

She groaned in response to his pinch and his strong words, her eyes closing as if the pain was her ultimate bliss. His cock thickened even more. He needed to take the edge off, find some semblance of relief or he was going to come in his pants like a fucking schoolboy.

"Get under the table," he commanded.

Her eyes flew open, her gaze questioning.

"I want you on your knees. Between my thighs. You're going to suck my cock until I come."

Caitlyn threw a glance toward the door. She was worried about the waiter. Her hesitance had no place here. He would protect her, and it was time she learned that lesson.

"Do it now, Cait."

She slipped from her chair with perfect grace. He parted his thighs, making room for her. For the briefest of moments, she didn't move. He didn't offer her any more instructions. Instead, he waited to see what she would do.

She started with his belt, unhooking it. Lucas took the buckle from her and slid the leather strap out completely as her hands rested on his thighs.

He couldn't see her, as she'd lifted the tablecloth to his waist, so she could reach his belt. It was probably stupid to cut his vision off, as he relied on his eyes to gauge her emotions, her responses. However, despite her inexperience, Caitlyn's confidence, her willingness to accept his commands, told him she was hungry for this.

She had her safe word, and he trusted she would use it if he pushed her too far, too fast.

He doubled the belt in half, lifted the tablecloth and laid it over his thigh. A symbol. A threat.

For a second, he considered lifting the tablecloth, wanting to see her reaction to the belt, but he realized vision wasn't the only sense he could rely on.

Caitlyn released a quiet, "oh," that solidified his belief that the woman kneeling between his legs was his sexual equal. The tone was pure arousal.

Which meant Caitlyn wasn't the only novice in the room. He'd never found a sub who matched his own desires so perfectly.

She must have anticipated he had plans for the belt. He did. But that wasn't going to happen here in the restaurant. That pleasure would have to wait until later.

"Cait." He let his single word, the harsh tone as he spoke her name, remind her of her task.

She unbuttoned and unzipped his pants, her hand reaching in to tug out his cock. For the first time, Lucas was grateful for the tablecloth between them. There was no way he could school his emotions, hide how much this encounter was impacting him when she took his dick in her hand and stroked it slowly.

Lucas swallowed his groan when he felt her hot breath against the head, a split second before she took it into her mouth. His hands clenched into fists as he forced himself to keep them on the table. He'd intended this first encounter to be a slow exploration. A way to test her willingness to submit, to force her out of her comfort zone and to help him relieve a bit of pressure at the same time.

Now, however, it was taking every ounce of strength he had not to grip her hair in his hands, pulling her on his cock deeper, harder. He wanted to fuck her mouth, to claim her in no uncertain terms, to prove to her that one night would never be enough for them.

Caitlyn moved slowly—too fucking slowly—and Lucas closed his eyes, forced air into his lungs as he fought to center himself. To recover.

A reflection in the window caught his eye.

He'd been expecting this.

Lucas reached beneath the table as the waiter entered the room. He cupped her head in one hand, pushing his cock deeper into her mouth.

"My date is in the ladies' room," he said, letting Caitlyn know they were no longer alone. As he expected, she stiffened and stilled.

That wasn't part of this plan. He closed his hand in her hair, using his firm hold on her long, soft tresses to guide her movements. He pulled her off his cock until only the head remained, then he pushed her back down on him.

She resisted his push and pull for one stroke. And then the beautiful, responsive woman submitted. Followed his lead, she gave him exactly what he'd silently demanded.

It was very likely the waiter knew exactly where his date was, but he kept his eyes on his task, clearing the plates and placing the next course in front of him with quick efficiency. Caitlyn sucked his cock in utter silence. An amazing feat considering the roaring white noise in his head that told him he wasn't going to last much longer.

Lucas shook his head when the waiter asked if he wanted his wineglass topped up. Mercifully, the man finished his tasks and moved on.

Once he was out of the room, Lucas reached beneath the tablecloth, using both hands to ramp up the pace and the force as he took Caitlyn's mouth.

She responded to the roughness, the utter claiming.

He was using her. He needed her. Had to fucking have her. On his terms.

"I'm going to come in your mouth," he said harshly.

Lucas didn't give her a chance to reply, though the way she moaned on his sensitive flesh told him she was ready.

He tightened his grip on her hair and pushed himself completely into her mouth. Caitlyn's throat opened as he slid straight to the back. It was exactly where he wanted to be. Come erupted as his balls constricted. He stiffened briefly, letting the sheer pleasure of this moment sweep through him.

Caitlyn didn't seek to pull away, her lips still wrapped around his softening cock. Once he'd recovered, he gently released her hair.

"Come back to the table, Cait."

As she slowly reemerged, Lucas tucked himself back into his pants, refastening them. He left the belt off for now.

He studied her flushed face, admiring the way she held his gaze. The way she looked at him with an almost confused expression.

God. She was on the verge of her own orgasm.

He pushed her skirt up and tugged her legs apart. "You want to come, Cait?"

She nodded, her hands reaching out for his arms. She gripped them tightly. "Please."

Lucas was tempted to give in to her plea. There was nothing he wanted more than to see her come. But tonight was about pushing her limits, proving that he was capable of giving her more than she even knew she wanted.

Rather than drive his fingers into her hot, wet pussy, he dipped them into his water glass, pulling out a chunk of ice.

Caitlyn shook her head when his intentions became clear. "No, Lucas. Please. I need your fingers inside me. Fuck me with them. Hard."

"Don't tell me what to do, Cait."

While she liked to pretend what she'd shared with Sammy was something like a D/s relationship, she was wrong.

"But—"

"Say one more word and this night ends here." He prayed to God she didn't push him on that threat.

Caitlyn opened her mouth, and then thankfully, she closed it again.

He rubbed the ice around her clit as she jerked, trying to move away from the extreme cold. "Hold still," he commanded, and though he saw her struggle to obey, she stopped moving. A shudder racked her slim frame.

Lucas ran the ice along her slit, provoking another shiver. Then he pushed the ice cube inside her.

"Close your legs."

She wanted to fight him. He could read the refusal on her lips. If she said no, Lucas wouldn't hesitate to pull her over his lap and put his belt to good use. While his mind told him he needed to slow down, every other part of him demanded that he make his sub obey.

Mine.

The word kept sneaking into his subconscious.

Slowly, Caitlyn drew her legs together.

Lucas picked up his fork and gestured toward hers. "Eat your dinner."

She broke off a bit of the jumbo crab cake with her fork, though it was obvious food was the last thing on her mind.

Just before she took the bite, he said, "Tell me when the ice has completely melted, so I can replace it."

Caitlyn closed her eyes, and he wondered if she was praying. Then he wondered what she might pray for.

Patience? Strength? Lightning to strike him dead?

They ate in silence for a few minutes, but Lucas missed her voice. Missed talking to her. Typically, once his dates moved into the sexual phase, he didn't bother with conversation, didn't need or want it.

With Caitlyn, he wanted her submission, her body, and a peek inside her fascinating mind.

"How do you feel right now?"

"Horny."

He laughed. Probably not the right response, given the way her eyes narrowed, but he didn't care. Lucas spent too much of his time around humorless, serious people who wouldn't get a joke if it bit them in the ass. People who looked at him with distrust or outright hate or even fear.

Caitlyn had a sarcastic wit that amused him more than he cared to admit.

"You think that's funny?"

Lucas leaned closer, cupping the back of her neck in one hand. She responded to the strong grip, just as he'd anticipated. "I think you're beautiful. Sexy. And yes. Funny."

"Tonight would be a lot easier for me if you didn't say nice things."

"I already told you. I don't want tonight to be easy for you."

"Lucas."

"Yes?"

"The ice has melted."

He didn't respond. Instead, he reached for another piece, pleased when she opened her legs without him prompting her to. This time, rather than simply slipping the ice in, he pushed two fingers with it. Her pussy clenched against them tightly.

It wouldn't take him more than a dozen thrusts to bring her to orgasm. They both knew it.

Caitlyn opened her mouth, but he cut her off with his lips on hers.

Until that point, he'd resisted kissing her. It was a danger.

One that he stopped caring about the second her lips parted and her tongue touched his. Lucas curled his fingers inside her, pushing the ice around, running the cold cube along every surface.

Caitlyn gasped and tried to pull back, but he didn't let her go. He kissed her harder, his tongue exploring her mouth the same way the ice traveled around her pussy.

She pushed at his shoulders, still intent on getting away. It was the first time she'd genuinely fought him. Her reaction to this kiss seemed to mirror his, but now that he'd taken a taste of her, he was throwing caution to the wind. He wanted more of her. All of her.

Lucas broke the connection of their lips briefly when she continued shoving him away. "Say your safe word or stop resisting."

For a moment, he thought she was going to say her word. It left him unnerved. She'd dropped to her knees beneath the table and let him fuck her mouth without a single complaint. Now, he was merely kissing her, and she was close to freaking out, running away.

Lucas stilled, then placed one soft, quick kiss on her lips before moving away.

Caitlyn's legs closed once more around the ice he'd left there. Lucas wiped his hand on his napkin and turned his attention back to his food, giving Caitlyn a chance to gather her wits.

"Explain," he said after a few quiet minutes.

"I don't think we should kiss anymore." She hadn't bothered to pick up her own fork. He'd spent a small fortune on tonight's meal. Clearly the money had been wasted. Neither of them was enjoying the food, too intent on what came after.

And suddenly he understood; knew why she wanted to keep him from kissing her. She was wise to resist, yet Lucas didn't like having limits set for him.

Caitlyn wanted to experience a night with a Dom, wanted to explore her submissiveness, yet she continued to try to call the shots.

And on top of that, she was still determined to keep him firmly in the villain category. She'd take what she wanted from him physically, trying to justify her actions as mere exploration. Emotionally, she would remain aloof, casting him in the role of bad guy. She wasn't the first person to see him that way, but for some inexplicable reason, it bothered him that she did.

Lucas rose from the table, unwilling to put off the inevitable. He'd warned her before that he wouldn't be controlled. She wouldn't top him from the bottom. It was time to prove to her exactly what that meant.

She'd already put one condition on him, demanding they only take this one night. Now she was attempting to restrict his kisses. He put his belt back on, tucked his shirt in, moving slowly, methodically as he tried to calm down.

Caitlyn remained seated, watching him warily. She was smart enough to see she'd pushed the wrong button, wise enough to remain quiet as he struggled to control his emotions.

"Stand up, Cait. We're leaving."

She didn't move. "You're taking me home?"

He nodded. "Yes."

She thought the date was over, thought she'd irritated him enough that he was calling the whole thing to a halt. He let her chew over that mistaken assumption for a couple minutes before reaching out to take her hand, drawing her up. He was relieved to see her disappointment.

"And when we get back to *my* home, you're going to take off all your clothes and kneel in front of me."

His words had the desired effect. Relief suffused her face at the knowledge the date wasn't over. That look eased some of the lingering anger he felt. While she still wanted to resist this, she wanted it—wanted him—more.

Lucas paid their bill, assuring the waiter their early departure had nothing to do with the quality of the food. The ride back to his place was made in silence. He let it linger on purpose, letting the anticipation—maybe even Caitlyn's trepidation and fear—grow.

The woman was too used to being in control. Of herself. Of her emotions. By taking kissing off the table, by putting the one-night time limit on this affair, she'd proven that she would submit to his demands only within the confines of her own desires.

He didn't bend to anyone's will. And he sure as shit didn't intend to start tonight.

He saw Caitlyn's anxiety increase when they pulled into the parking garage beneath his building.

Lucas owned the large, luxury apartments on the waterfront and he'd claimed the penthouse for himself.

He turned off the car and got out, demanding she wait for him.

Crossing around the Jag, he opened the passenger door and took her hand, leading her to the elevator. He pushed in the code that would lead to his place, and again he let the silence remain.

"Lucas," she started.

"Be quiet, Cait. I've told you what I want. If you're unwilling to submit, then say the word and I'll take you home."

She bit her lower lip, but didn't say anything more.

As the elevator doors slid open, they walked the short distance to his door. His was the only apartment on the floor. It provided him complete privacy, an oasis from the stress of his job, a retreat away from his parents, his colleagues, acquaintances and friends. This place was simply for him, and it was extremely rare for him to allow another to enter.

Once he opened the door, he stood aside as she walked inside. He watched Caitlyn's eyes widen. He knew exactly how impressive his home was. He'd designed it that way. One whole wall of the living room was floor-to-ceiling glass, leaving an unhindered view of the city lights flickering on the water of the Inner Harbor. From up here, he could look down on the city and feel like he owned the world.

A soft mew distracted Caitlyn. "Oh!" She bent down and picked up his cat before he could warn her. "Where did you come from?"

"Careful. She—" Lucas stopped mid-sentence, amazed when his typically mean-as-a-snake cat allowed

Caitlyn to not only pick her up, but flip her to her back and rub her stomach.

"Aren't you a sweet thing?" Caitlyn cooed at his cat, stroking her as Callie purred loudly. When Caitlyn's attention returned to him, he could see the genuine surprise in her expression. "I have to admit, I didn't see you as a cat person."

He shrugged, trying to downplay how much the silly little ball of fluff meant to him. "She's a stray. I found her down in the parking garage, more fleas than fur. I carried her up and fed her, intent on dropping her off at the animal shelter the next day. Obviously, that didn't happen. She's been here about six months and she's sort of proclaimed the penthouse her domain. She tolerates me, lets me live here," he joked.

Caitlyn smiled, clearly delighted by his story. "That's so sweet of you. What's her name?"

"I called her Calico at the beginning because as I said, I didn't really intend to keep her. It's been shortened to Callie since then. She doesn't like strangers as a rule, so you might want to be careful. She scratched and bit my housekeeper the first couple of times the woman came to clean. Now they grudgingly give each other a wide berth."

Caitlyn shrugged, unconcerned. "She's an absolute sweetheart."

Caitlyn nuzzled Callie, and Lucas enjoyed the image of her cuddling his cat. Then he saw her hand shake slightly, and he realized she was stalling. Time to start the game once more.

"Put the cat down, Cait."

And just like that, the tension returned. Caitlyn had pushed him too far in the restaurant.

He'd told her what he wanted from her, but she remained still. Caitlyn looked at him nervously before she finally bent to return Callie to the floor. When she stood up again, she made no move to undress.

"I don't like to be kept waiting."

He was pushing her too hard. If he kept up this aggressiveness, she would throw the safe word at him and leave.

Or so he thought.

Until Caitlyn turned her back to him and lifted her dress over her head, giving him a generous glimpse of her bare ass as she slipped off her heels. She wore thigh-high stockings, and for a second he considered telling her to leave them on. They were sexy as fuck on her trim legs. He reconsidered that command when she bent over to roll them off.

Her ass was begging for his hand. His belt. Before the night ended, he fully intended to show her exactly what happened to a submissive who resisted her Dom's control.

Her back was still to him. She had to know that position would displease him. However, rather than correct her, he waited to see what she would do next.

Within moments, her bra joined the rest of her clothing piled up on the floor.

And then she turned.

Her hands remained at her sides as she let him look his fill. Once again, he was taken in by her confidence. She was beautiful. And she knew it. Not in a showy, stuck-up sense. More like she had enough self-esteem to say, "I love who I am, flaws and all, and you can take it or leave it."

Someone had instilled a strong sense of self-worth in her.

He was glad.

And then he was undone.

Caitlyn slid to her knees, parting them before resting her palms on her thighs face up. She'd done her homework. What she lacked in practical application, the intelligent woman had made up for in academic study.

Lucas stood there, taking in the image for several minutes. Through it all, Caitlyn kept her eyes downward, and he sensed this moment was as powerful for her as it was for him.

Unable to resist touching her, he walked over and cupped her cheek, guiding her face up until she was looking at him.

Submitting to someone was as mental as it was physical. He wanted to make sure Caitlyn understood that. "Who does your body belong to?"

She didn't hesitate. "You." And then, because Caitlyn still wasn't finished fighting this—him—she quietly added, "For now."

With those two words, she sealed her fate. He reached down, gripping her upper arms to pull her to a stand. Retaining his firm hold on one arm, he tugged her toward a chair near the window. Within seconds, he had her facedown over his lap.

Shock had allowed him to get her into the position fairly easily, but her stunned acquiescence was brief. Caitlyn pushed against his leg, intent on rising. He stopped her escape with a firm smack on her bare ass.

"Ouch!"

He spanked her again. And then again.

He didn't feel the need to give her a chance to accommodate or adjust. She knew how to stop this, knew what to say. Unless or until she said the safe word, he was going to show her exactly who she belonged to.

And not just for now.

"I'm going to kiss you, Caitlyn."

She had stopped trying to escape, her ass actually lifting in anticipation of his spanking, until he spoke.

"No."

Lucas froze for a moment, her refusal shaking his calm. He would never hit a woman in anger. Though, when he considered it, it wasn't anger he felt. At least not the way she might think. He didn't give a shit that she was saying no to him. He was more upset that she was denying herself something that she clearly, desperately wanted.

He leaned back in the chair and unfastened his belt, slipping it from the loops once more. Caitlyn's ass was pink from his spanking. Her breathing was heavy and loud in the quiet room. She cried out when he doubled the leather belt and dragged it along her sore bottom.

"I'm not going to respond to the word no, Cait."

She looked up at him, her lips pressed firmly closed.

"I am going to kiss you. All night."

She shook her head, but she didn't say the safe word.

"What do you want?" he asked, knowing perfectly well how she'd reply.

"The belt," she choked out.

Caitlyn wanted it, craved the pain, took immense pleasure in the sting, the bite. He'd give it to her. Jesus, he wanted it as much as she did. But not yet. Not until he'd made her understand what true submission meant.

He gripped her arm with his free hand and twisted her until she was cradled in his lap. She winced, the spanking still fresh, still sore.

"I'm going to kiss you," he repeated. She wasn't going to get what she wanted until he got his.

Tears formed in the corners of her eyes. She'd take his commands, his belt, his rough touches, but not his kisses.

Lucas refused to be denied. If she couldn't bend on this, it was over. It would kill him to do it, but he would take her home and that would be it.

He cupped her face in his hand. "I'm going to kiss you." He tightened his grip to keep her from shaking her head again. Then he bent toward her and kissed her. Softly. Gently.

There was no doubt she preferred a rougher kiss. A more demanding one.

She proved that when she bit his tongue. Hard.

He jerked away, but rather than respond the way she wanted, he pressed his lips against her cheek, sliding his mouth along the soft skin to her ear. He worshiped her with his lips, his mouth, his tongue.

Caitlyn gripped his hair and pulled it, hard enough to make his scalp sting. He only gentled the kiss more, lightly sucking her earlobe into his mouth, teasing the tiny bit of flesh with his tongue.

"Damn it, Lucas! Stop it."

"No."

She'd spoken every word except one. The one guaranteed to push him away. That told him that as much as she wanted to resist feeling something for him other than disdain, she was weakening. Starting to see him as something other than a monster.

He'd lived a lifetime as LexLuthor. Lucas sort of liked the idea of playing Superman for once.

She released his hair and gripped his shirt, tearing it apart with a surprising amount of strength. Buttons flew, the material ripped. If she was trying to provoke a response, she was going about it the wrong way. Her actions were starting to amuse him. And God help him, turn him on. He'd dealt with brats before.

Caitlyn moved toward his chest, biting him. It fucking hurt.

He wrapped his fingers in her hair and pulled her face away from his chest, bent lower until they were eye to eye. "I'm going to kiss you."

This time, his words appeared to sink in. And take the wind out of her sails.

"I need this to be just tonight. Just sex."

He grinned, even though he felt no humor. He'd lived his entire life having "just sex." He was the master of it. In truth, if he were thinking clearly, he'd give her what she was asking for. Because it wouldn't just keep her safe. It would protect him too.

If he were a braver man, he would have spoken the truth. He would have said no to her request. But if he did that, she'd give him the safe word. He knew that with the same certainty he had that this affair wasn't going to end as easily as all his previous ones.

Two words could end it all right now. Before either of them got in too deep.

All he had to say was no.

All she had to say was blue.

Neither of them spoke.

Instead, he stood up with Caitlyn in his arms and carried her to his bedroom.

Mari Carr

Chapter Five

Caitlyn was torn between running and begging. If she had an ounce of self-preservation, she'd say her safe word and get the hell out of here. After all, the whole night had been one big fucked-up mistake. She'd lied to her family about her reasons for going out with Lucas, claiming she was merely playing spy.

In truth, she'd gone out with him because she wanted what he could give her. Wanted it so badly, it nearly consumed her.

Living so many years as an unfulfilled submissive had taken its toll on her. So much so, she was throwing herself into the arms of the enemy.

That would be fine if she could keep her emotions contained, but Caitlyn was a Wallace *and* a Collins, which meant her genetic makeup was a dangerous blend of passion, insanity, falling fast, and stubbornness, laced with a healthy need for wild adventure.

Fool that she was, she thought she'd beat those attributes into submission, willed them away by sheer determination. In just a few hours, Lucas had proved she didn't have anything under control.

Not. One. Damn. Thing.

Least of all, this overwhelming attraction that was creeping out of the physical realm and into something a hell of a lot more dangerous. She was starting to like Lucas Whiting. Like *really* like him. He wasn't at all what she'd expected.

Well, that wasn't entirely true. The guy was cocky, overbearing, selfish, rich as fuck—she still couldn't quite believe the utter grandeur of this penthouse apartment—and far too used to getting his own way.

But there was more there. Stuff that didn't bother her, that actually tugged at her heartstrings and made her feel sympathy for him.

Like the way he'd clearly loved and grieved for his brother, the part of him that had suffered under a cruel father and indifferent mother, the indescribable look in his eyes that told her he was probably very lonely, the fact that he took in a stray cat.

God. That damn cat had thrown her for a loop.

And more than that, he had a sense of humor, a pretty cool laugh, an intellect that seemed well suited to hers, and his kisses. Holy mother of macaroni. His kisses were something entirely out of this world. Heavenly.

So, instead of squirming out of his hold and running for the hills, Caitlyn had tightened her grip around his neck and let him carry her to his bedroom. Like the damsel in distress she was about to become.

Once they entered the room, he put her on her feet and stood behind her, her back pressed against his chest. She felt sort of bad for destroying his shirt. She was sure it cost a fortune.

"Sorry about your shirt," she murmured.

"Don't worry about it."

"I can replace it."

"It's Armani and cost five hundred dollars."

"Or maybe I could just sew the buttons back on."

He chuckled. It was hard to hold on to her guilt when Lucas wrapped his arm around her waist and tugged her tighter. She could feel his rock-hard abs against her back. The man was carved of stone—a Greek Adonis come to life.

"It's okay, Caitlyn."

His bedroom, not surprisingly, was elegantly decorated and screamed of wealth. She was fairly certain she could fit her family's entire second-floor apartment in just this room, and she'd never seen a bigger four-poster bed in her life. "Do you need a GPS to find your way out of that bed every morning?"

Rather than reply to her jest, Lucas kissed the side of her neck and her eyes drifted closed.

Hello, erogenous zone.

She sighed.

"Go stand beside the bed, Cait. Keep your back to me."

Caitlyn's body was moving before her brain could engage, could consider her actions with sound, well-thought-out reasoning.

Apparently, wisdom wasn't happening tonight. She was working with the visceral rather than the intellectual.

Once she reached the bed, she couldn't resist touching the silky, soft comforter. The room was decorated in dark blues, similar to his shirt. She would have pegged him as a starker black-and-white guy, so she was pleasantly surprised by the rich, deep color.

She jumped slightly when something flashed over her head. She reached up as Lucas secured a blindfold over her eyes.

"Lucas?"

"Shhh. The safe word is still there to protect you." He pressed her forward, encouraging her to climb onto the bed.

"Lay on your back. Lift your arms above your head," he instructed as he guided her into the position he wanted.

Lucas knelt next to her. She wasn't surprised when he buckled her wrists to the corner posts with straps. This bed was made for bondage.

Her other senses were heightened by her lack of vision. She would have expected the utter blackness to be unnerving, but it was fueling her arousal, turning her on even more. A response she didn't think possible, considering she was practically on system overload. The ice at the restaurant had done nothing to cool her needs.

Between Lucas's commands, the kneeling, the spanking and the way she still wanted to feel his leather belt against her ass, she was one light breeze away from coming hard enough to break bones.

The bondage worked its magic. "God, Lucas. Please. Please fuck me. My whole body hurts."

She felt him move over her. Bastard still had his pants on. And the shirt. The ripped sides tickled her as he leaned closer, his lips hovering at her ear.

"Telling me what to do only ensures that I won't."

She was starting to figure that out. Even so... "Yeah, so I noticed. You realize leaving a girl hanging for this long is kind of a dick move."

"I thought the fact I was a dick was well established already."

"I thought we'd established asshole." She didn't appear to be winning this battle. And there was something in his tone that made her think maybe she'd hurt his feelings. "You're not a complete dick," she said, hoping to make him laugh.

He didn't, but there was definite humor in his tone when he said, "High praise. Cait?"

"Yeah?"

"Stop talking or I'll gag you too."

Caitlyn bit her lip, seriously tempted to go for that. She only had tonight, and she really wanted to experience everything. The idea of a gag had her pussy clenching. Regardless, she held her tongue. She was already blindfolded and bound. If he added a gag to the mix, in addition to being completely helpless, she'd probably spontaneously combust.

"Good girl," he murmured when it was apparent she was going to obey. He placed a soft kiss on her cheek before drifting lower.

He stroked her neck with his tongue, and then settled at her breasts. The gentle tenor he'd begun in the living room vanished and her dominant lover was back.

Hallelujah.

Rough, she could handle.

He grasped one breast in his hand, kneading the flesh roughly, pinching her nipple, while his teeth sank into the other. He sucked, bit, pinched. He also caressed, licked and stroked. Every shard of pain he produced was soothed away.

For several minutes, he guided her back and forth between pain and pleasure until she was gasping, crying and, despite his threat to gag her, begging him for mercy. And then for more.

"Your tits are perfect," he muttered. "Take a deep breath and hold it."

She didn't have a clue what to expect, but she did as he said.

"Shit," she cried out when he placed the first nipple clamp in place. She didn't need her eyes to know that was what he was using. She'd bought a pair for herself several years earlier. At first, she'd toyed with them on her own, using them whenever she masturbated. Then she'd shown them to Sammy, who'd told her they looked hot on her.

Lucas wielded them with a hell of a lot more power.

He didn't seem to acknowledge or care about her cursing because he snapped the second clamp in place without hesitation. The chain that hung between them tickled her belly.

"Oh my God." She thrashed her head against the pillow, fighting against the straps around her wrists for the first time.

"Have you ever considered having your nipples pierced?"

She had. She'd even made an appointment to have it done once. But she'd backed out at the last minute.

"I...yes," she admitted.

Lucas didn't reply, and for the first time since he'd cinched the blindfold in place, she wished it were gone. She wanted to see his face, his eyes, wanted to know what he was thinking, feeling. He tugged on the chain a couple of times, gauging her reactions. And he got them.

Caitlyn was slowly losing control. Which was obviously the point. She'd never felt like this. She was walking on a tightrope without a net. Or even one of those long poles for balance.

"Take off the blindfold. Please."

"No."

He paused briefly, and she wondered if he was considering reaching for the gag. While she'd thought that sounded hot at first, she was starting to panic.

Lucas ran his hand along her hair. "Breathe."

She sucked in one deep breath and then another. Lucas ran his fingers around the clamps, but he didn't tug on the chain, didn't seek to increase the pleasure or the pain.

After a few minutes, she managed to calm down. She tried to imagine Lucas's face, tried to envision what he might be seeing. She didn't want him to stop.

Caitlyn slowly centered herself and did the one thing she'd never managed to do in her life. She cleared everything out—work, family, fear, stress—and simply felt.

Her breasts were hot, on fire, and she could feel that fever spreading to other parts of her body. She bent her knees slightly and wished he'd tied her ankles to the bed as well. Strange as it sounded, there was freedom in the restraints. It was as if she could write off all responsibility for once. She could say "I couldn't move so whatever happened wasn't up to me."

That wasn't true. She only had to say "blue" and Lucas would stop. She wasn't sure where that assurance came from, that utter trust. After all, they were practically strangers. Regardless, there was something about him that told her he was a man of his word.

Letting go was incredible. It felt as if everything was always up to her, and she was so fucking tired. A tension she didn't realize was there loosened in her shoulders and vanished, and her breathing slowed, deepened.

"Beautiful," Lucas whispered.

Had he noticed the change in her? Recognized that the fight was over? What would she give to see those piercing, intense, sexy eyes of his? She didn't have long to regret the loss of her vision when he moved lower, his tongue traveling along her stomach to her pussy.

He parted her with his thumbs and lost no time sucking her clit into his mouth. He treated the sensitive nub to the same treatment he'd just given her nipples— nips, sucks, bites, the rough stroking of his tongue.

Caitlyn's body tingled. She could almost imagine it shimmering like the lights on the water outside.

Lucas moved even lower, running his tongue along her slit from ass to clit and back again. His fingers moved toward her pussy and he pressed two inside.

Her heels dug into the mattress as she lifted her ass, seeking more pressure.

Lucas halted her attempts by grasping her legs, pulling her knees over his shoulders. It opened her even farther, but gave her precious little opportunity to move. He added a third finger and drove in harder. Her back arched.

"Next time, I'm using rope. I'm restricting all your movement."

She hissed the word "yes" even as her head screamed *there won't be a next time.*

Tonight.

Only tonight.

She fought to remember that. To keep it front and center. It was becoming more and more impossible with each passing minute.

Lucas knew too much about her desires. As he revealed them, each hidden piece was moved out of the inky-black darkness and into the light. If they kept going, if she came back for another night, and another, there was no way he wouldn't eventually see it all.

He pulled his fingers out of her pussy, and she sighed with relief. She needed him to fuck her. So badly.

However, it appeared playtime wasn't over when Lucas pushed one finger into her anus. It was wet from the juices of her pussy, so his entrance was made easier. He thrust it in three times, and then he added a second finger.

It was a tight fit and it pinched. She liked it. He wasn't gentle, didn't treat her with kid gloves, didn't constantly ask if she was okay or seek permission. Somehow she trusted that he'd know if she wasn't all right, and there was freedom in that too.

Lucas drove his fingers in faster. Caitlyn was only vaguely aware of the sounds coming from her lips—the grunts, the groans, the cries, the pleas.

For more. For harder. For faster.

"I'm going to stretch this tight little ass with a plug. Then I'm going to fuck it."

"Do it," she demanded. "God, please."

As always, Lucas pushed her right to the brink, and then he left her there teetering for balance. The bastard refused to give her a shove over.

When she heard him chuckle, she realized she'd called him a bastard aloud. His amused response fired her temper.

"Oh my God. You're an asshole *and* a dick. Fuck me. Fuck me now!"

One minute she was in utter darkness, the next, light. While Lucas's room was somewhat dim, the only light provided by the lamp across the room and the city lights below, she hadn't expected him to pull the blindfold off.

She blinked, trying to focus her vision, but all she could see was Lucas's blurry face mere inches from her.

"Are you finished?"

He was pissed? Seriously?

She opened her mouth to remind him that he'd already come tonight, but he kissed her, roughly.

"Hold your breath," he demanded, mere seconds before he released the first nipple clamp.

Shards of pain shot through her, and her pussy clenched. She pressed her legs together, wishing he were inside her.

He released the other, and then he suckled them, soothed them with his gentle tongue and his warm breath. All the time, her inner muscles throbbed looking for something, anything to fill her body.

She had wanted her vision earlier, thinking she'd understand Lucas's feelings better if she could see him. She'd been wrong. His face revealed more than she wanted to see.

He wasn't going to let her walk out of here tonight, wasn't finished with her.

If he took her now, everything was going to change. Everything.

"I should go," she whispered.

"No. You shouldn't." Lucas opened the nightstand drawer and pulled out a condom. Caitlyn wanted to cry with relief that he was finally going to take her—and then with fear. She was in so far over her head, there was no hope she'd survive this.

Her heart, which had slowed, resumed its racing pace, thudding so hard it almost hurt.

"The safe word is still there, Cait."

Blue.

Blue.

Blue.

The word wouldn't come. "I don't want to say it."

"Good. Because I don't want to hear it." Lucas rose from the bed, stripping off his pants. He'd lost the shirt and his shoes at some point while she was blindfolded. Once the condom was in place, he returned to the bed. He undid the straps at her wrists. She was glad. She wanted to touch him.

He resumed his place above her and placed the head of his cock at her entrance. Lucas paused.

She sensed he wanted to say something, but she was afraid to ask what. Mainly because she could see it in his eyes.

He wanted to explore more of these submissive tendencies of hers. He'd mentioned rope and a butt plug, the gag, pierced nipples. And there was that leather belt.

But it felt like there was something more there as well. Something that had nothing to do with sex.

Caitlyn reached up and cupped his cheek in her hand. It was a tender gesture, one laced with more feeling than she was smart to allow.

"Come inside me," she whispered. "Please."

Lucas turned his lips toward her palm and placed a soft kiss on it.

And then he was there, seated to the hilt after one hard, deep thrust.

Her head flew back against the pillow, her legs wrapped around his waist. Whatever restraints had been holding both of them back were gone. In this, they knew what they wanted and they took it. Gave it.

After a few minutes, Lucas rolled to his back, pulling her on top. She straddled his hips and found her own pounding pace.

Lucas twisted her still-sore nipples, adding just the right amount of pain to throw her into overload once more. When she was on the verge of coming, he lifted her off his cock, despite her protestations.

Her curses ceased the second he tossed her facedown on the mattress and grasped her wrists, tugging them behind her back.

"Get up on your knees," he demanded.

She bent her legs, her ass rising. Lucas kept hold of her hands in one of his as he used the other to guide his cock back inside her. She screamed at the force behind his motions. It was so deep this way.

"So fucking good," she cried.

Their skin was slick with sweat from their exertions. Her wrists slipped out of his grasp, so he moved to her hair. Gripping a large handful, he used it to pull her chest from the bed until her back was upright, pressed against him. Through it all, he pounded inside her, reaching around to stroke her clit.

Her scalp stung and her pussy tightened. She saw stars. Her orgasm struck hard and fast and painfully. He'd kept her on the edge for hours and her body was pissed, taking every ounce of pleasure it could soak up, tired of being denied.

She shook roughly and expected Lucas to come as well.

"Fuck," he said through gritted teeth. She could only imagine what her orgasm must feel like against his dick. Even to her, it seemed vise-tight. Was she hurting him?

As the final ripples of her orgasm began to wane, Lucas loosened his grip on her hair, letting her collapse face-first back to the bed. Despite her sudden stillness, he continued to thrust inside her, though his motions were slower, easier.

Every now and then, her body trembled with an aftershock, and she was beginning to give up all hope of ever catching her breath again.

And still Lucas was there, his cock stroking all the uber-sensitive places. On one retreat, he withdrew completely.

"Roll over, Cait. I want to see your face."

Grace was gone. She turned from her stomach to her back like a woman devoid of bones and muscles. She probably looked more like a fish flopping on the shore.

Lucas pressed her legs open, and she sucked in a harsh gasp of air as he pushed inside once more. He came over her, his elbows resting on the mattress.

And then he kissed her. More of those soft, sweet, beautiful kisses that messed up her head and her heart and had her thinking romantic, mushy things that had no place in this bed.

She'd tried to warn him, to tell him that kissing was a bad thing, but he'd taken her words as a dare, a challenge. The man was too competitive for his own good. And Caitlyn was nothing if not a hopeless romantic.

Caitlyn turned her head to the side, determined to make him understand this time. "Please, Lucas. I can't—"

"I'm not going to be the villain in your life story."

She frowned as she looked at him, confused by the resolve in his gaze. "What?"

Lucas slowed his thrusting even more, but as they spoke, Caitlyn didn't forget he was there, filling her, taking her in a way that was just as powerful—maybe more so—as their fast-paced, rough fucking.

"Kiss me, Cait."

He waited for her to initiate it, but she couldn't. Couldn't he see that? She wasn't the type of woman who could turn her feelings off and on like a faucet. When they kissed, she felt...something dangerous. Scary. Something that would definitely strip her of all control.

When she didn't move, his face hardened, not with anger, but with determination. "I'm not just a cock for you to play with. And I'm not a dick. I'm a man. And you *are* going to kiss me."

He shoved her out into the light completely, seeing not only what she was, but what she thought he was.

A one-night stand. A chance to explore her fantasies with a heartless man. The asshole trying to steal the pub. She'd pigeonholed him in all those boxes because she believed that would keep her safe.

All it had done was hurt him.

"I've been a selfish bitch," she whispered.

He shook his head. "If that were true, I wouldn't still be inside you."

Caitlyn lifted her head and kissed him. It was a quick, soft, almost platonic kiss, but it seemed to be enough. When her head returned to the pillow, Lucas followed her, deepening the kiss as he started thrusting harder.

She clung to his shoulders, and then ran her fingers through his thick hair. Lucas framed her face with his large palms, his tongue stroking hers as he moved faster.

They continued to kiss, their faces only parting when they reached the peak together.

"Caitlyn." Lucas called out her name as he came, his climax triggering another in her.

Neither of them moved for several minutes.

Lucas was the first to rouse.

"Back in a minute." He rose from the bed and disappeared into the master bath. She listened as he cleaned up, but reality crashed in quick.

Soon the pounding of her heart, the blood thudding in her ears, drowned out everything else.

She'd made a mistake of epic proportion.

Caitlyn forced herself to sit up and then to stand, even though her legs were shaky. Glancing around the room, she realized her clothes were still in the living room, on the floor where she'd dropped them after stripping for Lucas.

Why had she thought she could have sex with the man and not feel anything for him? How many times had she listened to her aunts and uncles talk about meeting their significant others? How many times had she been told that when a Collins falls in love, they fall hard and fast? Passionately. Recklessly. Irrationally.

She had tried to force those feelings with her previous boyfriends, insisting what she felt was that same love her parents shared. How many times had her mother told her to stop trying so hard? How many times had she warned Caitlyn that when it was right, when she found the one, she would know?

Lucas wasn't the one. He couldn't be.

Padding down the hallway, she'd only just managed to get her bra on—despite her shaking hands—when Lucas found her.

"What are you doing?"

"I need to get home."

"Caitlyn—"

He was going to fight her on this. She couldn't let him.

"I told you, Lucas. One night. This could only ever be one night." She hated how high-pitched her voice was, despised the outright panic in her tone.

He looked at her for an uncomfortably long minute and then he nodded. "Let me get dressed. I'll drive you."

"Uber would be easier."

"I'm driving you home, Caitlyn."

She let him have that battle. Only because it seemed like the quickest way for her to get out of here.

She tugged on her stockings, dress and shoes and was standing by the door when Lucas returned. He'd pulled on the same pants he wore earlier, but given the wreckage she'd wrought on his shirt, he had found a plain black T-shirt to wear instead. She would have preferred anything else, as the T-shirt accentuated his muscles, his beautiful chest, his sexy build.

Caitlyn turned her head. Looking at him wasn't helping.

Lucas picked up his keys and held out his hand. "Ready?"

She nodded, walking by his outstretched fingers. Touching wasn't any more advisable than looking. He frowned, clearly displeased to have his offer ignored.

Good. Perhaps her rude actions would help burn down the bridge between them, make it impossible for her to cross back over.

They rode in silence and she was grateful for the reprieve, his easy acceptance of their deal.

Perhaps he was even glad she was upholding it, and his apparent annoyance was based on the fact he'd had to drive her home tonight rather than in the morning.

Caitlyn's mind whirled as she tried to come to grips with so many warring emotions. It felt like twenty years had passed since she'd left home a few hours earlier.

As they pulled up in front of the pub, Caitlyn reached for the door handle, ready to sprint from the vehicle.

"Thanks for—"

Lucas grasped her wrist firmly, halting her escape. "Three days."

"What?"

"I'm giving you three days to get your shit together. To figure out and accept something that you already know, even if you don't want to admit it."

Caitlyn lifted her chin, trying to give the appearance of a boldness she didn't feel. "And what's that?"

"This isn't over. Not by a long shot."

Chapter Six

Lucas sat with his back to his office door, to his desk, to his computer. Hell, he'd turned his back on everything except the view from his twenty-fifth-floor window.

He was on day two of three, and kicking himself for giving Caitlyn so much time. Actually he never should have driven her home that night to begin with. If he'd been thinking clearly, he would have dragged her back to his bed, tied her to it and fucked her until she realized...

Realized what?

The answer to that question was why he'd driven her home. He had been just as confused, just as blindsided as she'd been. Lucas didn't do relationships. He didn't do commitment. And he sure as fuck didn't do love.

Yet every fiber of his being told him he could very easily do all three of those things with Caitlyn. So he was smart to put some distance and time between them. At least, that's what he'd been telling himself for the past—he glanced at his watch—thirty-seven hours.

"Where do we stand on the Sunnyside project?"

Lucas spun his chair toward the door and his father's voice. "I spoke to the foreman. They're two days behind schedule due to the weather."

Dad scowled. "Tell him to make that time up or it's coming out of his paycheck. What about the Collins building acquisition?"

The idea to purchase the building that housed Pat's Pub, the accompanying restaurant and apartment above had been Lucas's idea. Actually, the plan for that whole city block had been his. His father had actually tried to talk him out of the acquisition, claiming the area wasn't lucrative enough. Lucas had insisted, and then persevered. He was very convincing when he wanted something and he'd done his work well. His father was now one hundred percent behind the purchase, which meant Caitlyn's family had a snowball's chance in hell of holding on to their business.

"I'm still in talks with the owners."

His dad frowned. "What the hell does that mean? Did you make an offer?"

Lucas nodded. "I made the initial one. They refused."

"Everyone refuses the first. What did they say when you countered?"

And this was where the shit was about to hit the fan. "I haven't countered yet."

Dad's face reddened as he walked into his office, not stopping until he loomed above Lucas's desk. Julius Whiting was a prime candidate for a heart attack, given his poor eating habits, stress levels and high blood pressure. Yet, none of that was impetus enough for him to scale back or strive for a healthier lifestyle. "What the hell are you waiting for?"

Lucas had considered this conversation nonstop since dropping Caitlyn off in front of the pub night before last. "I'm beginning to think you were right about that area. I'm not sure it's financially profitable for us to pursue building there. It's more rundown than I realized and the surrounding neighborhoods are rough." Every word was a lie, and his father knew it.

They'd begun plans for gentrifying the area over a year earlier, and they'd made major inroads toward securing several of the other properties on the street. Whiting Properties intended to close down the current businesses, replacing them with high-end retail shops, creating a mirror image of Rodeo Drive in Baltimore.

The two buildings they'd purchased were already in the process of getting much-needed facelifts. The beauty parlor was going to become a Red Door Salon and Spa, ready to cater to a more sophisticated clientele. The pawnshop next door was about to be torn down to accommodate the spa part of the salon.

Next on their list was Pat's Irish Pub. Plans were in place to gut the building and put in an exclusive French restaurant similar to Maison Pic in Paris. Lucas had actually been meeting with the architects they'd hired to design the new restaurant in the pub the night he met Caitlyn.

The first time he'd walked into Pat's Pub, he had been surprised to discover it was even more charming on the inside than the out. It was the quaint setup out front that had caught Lucas's eye one day when his limo had passed by and inspired his gentrification plans. He'd taken one look at the pub and known he wanted it. And for six months, he'd done his research on the Collins family, set up his chess pieces and organized the game plan for acquisition.

Then he'd met Caitlyn Wallace, and the game board had been upended.

"We're gutting the building, Lucas. This is the beginning phase in a multi-year project. We've already grabbed three of the surrounding properties. They become worthless without the restaurant. You know that. So why don't you tell me what this is really about?" His father's voice grew louder and angrier as he spoke.

"I think we'd be smarter to take another look at that area on the east end again before we continue to snatch up more property in the pub neighborhood. That abandoned warehouse on the east end takes up the entire city block. One purchase and it's done. And it's in a better location for our plans. We can think of something else to do with those other small properties near the pub. Or we can off-load them."

His father's eyes narrowed and he leaned over the desk. "What the fuck is wrong with you? We've spent months and countless man-hours researching and planning this acquisition, not to mention the money we've already spent. We're not dropping it. We're not starting over."

Lucas felt compelled to remind his father that this had been his project from the outset, but that argument, like his previous ones, would fall on deaf ears.

Dad lifted his finger. "If you can't bring this deal home, I'll find someone else who can."

It was an empty threat and they both knew it. Lucas was the driving force when it came to acquisitions. It was what he did best.

His father's strengths lie in greasing the wheels and cozying up to those in power.

Lucas crunched the numbers, made the offers, and closed the deals. If he ran into any issues, he had his father's connections in his back pocket, although he tried hard not to call in those favors unless necessary. Mainly because his father—who oversaw construction and renovations once the properties had been acquired—sorely abused his connections with the power players when it came to zoning and building-code laws.

"I'm taking care of it."

"I want that property by the end of the month." His father walked away without another word. Lucas had learned a very long time ago to simply let his old man have the last word. It made life a hell of a lot easier.

Lucas glanced at the folder on his desk. It contained information he'd gathered on the Collins family over the past few months. It was the reason he'd turned his back on his desk earlier, opting for the view of the city.

Flipping open the folder, he saw a sketch of the Collins family tree his assistant had drawn up for him. They were a large brood, and with so many members of the family actively working in the pub, he'd spent quite a bit of time trying to piece out who was who, analyzing who might be most amenable to his offer, searching for a weak link.

What he'd found had been quite unlike anything he'd ever uncovered in past acquisitions. Typically, families with a successful business or property or even a little bit of money found ways to argue over it. Someone was always scrambling to grab the bigger piece of the pie.

That didn't seem to hold true when it came to the Collins clan. When Patrick Collins decided to retire from the business and move in with his daughter, Riley, he divided the business into eight equal portions, giving one to each of his children while retaining an eighth for himself. When he passed away, the seven siblings would then divide the business by seven.

It was a simple setup that should have been fraught with problems. Four of the seven siblings worked in the pub. Caitlyn's mom, Keira, and Ewan ran the restaurant, where Riley served as the cook. Meanwhile, Tristan took care of the pub side. The other siblings were silent partners with their own careers. Teagan was touring with her husband, Sky Mitchell, and Killian and Sean Collins ran a construction business with Killian's life partner, Justin.

There were a lot of fingers in the pie, especially when he figured in the next generation. In addition to his seven children, Patrick had twelve grandchildren. More than a handful of them were now involved in the business too, and over half of them lived on the second floor of the building. It wasn't natural for a family to be that close-knit, that tight. Yet it seemed to work for the Collinses.

Whiting Properties was made up of him and his father, and not a day passed where Lucas wasn't aware of the fact that was one Whiting too many. He couldn't begin to imagine working in a business with so many equal voices.

It should have been a simple matter for him to find the one disgruntled family member who wanted out. The one looking to make a quick buck, cut and run.

That hadn't been the case.

Lucas had walked in, made his offer, and within seconds the wagons had circled, shotguns aimed in his direction, and he was left on the outside with no hope of breaking through.

After his initial defeat, he bided his time, did more reconnaissance, turned his attention away from the siblings and concentrated on the next generation. The twelve of them were all in their early twenties to early thirties, Caitlyn the oldest. He'd expected to find at least one of them with some sort of vice he could exploit—a drug problem, gambling debts, legal troubles. And again, he came up empty.

Except for Caitlyn.

He turned the pages until he found the picture his assistant had included with Caitlyn's dossier. It was a professional portrait taken fairly recently that she used on the brochure to advertise the law firm she ran with Colm. He'd looked at that picture more often than he cared to admit prior to meeting her, and no less than a thousand times in the past two days.

Caitlyn.

A riddle wrapped in an enigma and buried within the most beautiful woman he'd ever laid eyes on.

She was independent and confident, yet at times she was as wary and scared as a kitten cornered by dogs.

She was fiercely loyal and devoted to her family which meant they would always be on opposite sides as long as the battle for the pub remained. His father wouldn't be swayed from the acquisition, which meant it fell to Lucas to find a way to make the deal more appealing to Caitlyn's family.

Her sexuality was a perfect mirror image to his. Her submissive tendencies were in direct counterpoint to his dominant needs. She didn't want a master any more than he wanted a slave. Typically, he had no problem separating sex from emotion, but that line had been blurred with Caitlyn.

He had actually believed he could take her home, issue a bunch of commands, bring them both to a pleasurable conclusion, and then convince her to continue the affair. He thought his feelings would never become engaged.

Why the hell would he think they would be? They'd never reared their ugly head in the past.

Because the women he'd dated had always reminded him too much of his mother. Women who valued the wealth and prestige he offered. Caitlyn wasn't interested in either.

He'd been touched by the compassion she'd shown when they talked about his brother's death. He'd been flattered by the genuine interest she'd shown in getting to know him better. He'd been amused by her wit. The woman was seriously funny. People didn't joke around with him. Probably because they assumed he was like his dad—humorless, intense, angry.

Sycophants surrounded him day in and day out. Caitlyn didn't bow down, didn't want anything from him. She was a challenge. With her, he felt a strong desire to prove himself, to earn her respect, her submission, her trust. To be on the receiving end of that same goddamned unwavering loyalty she gave to her family.

He wanted her to like him.

Even though he knew it was right for Caitlyn to walk away. He knew that as surely as he knew he was going to be knocking on her door tomorrow night.

For the first time in his life, Lucas didn't have a plan. He was walking blindly into a deal with no currency, no reserves on the bench and very little hope of winning.

And he was still going to knock on her door.

* * *

"Feel like some company for dinner? It's my break time."

Caitlyn looked up and tried to muster a smile for her mom. "Sure."

She'd come home from work half an hour earlier, but couldn't summon the energy to climb the stairs to her apartment. Probably because, while she'd been subjected to the third degree about her date from four of her cousins, there were still too many to go. They'd managed to pull together for her intervention prior to the date, but they'd made no effort to rally afterwards. Which meant she'd had to answer the same questions every time one of her cousins managed to catch up with her.

It was getting harder to pretend that nothing of significance had happened and that she'd come up empty-handed with her spying.

Mom placed the dinner special—shepherd's pie—in front of her and then claimed the other side of the booth.

"You're not eating?" Caitlyn asked.

"Your dad is stopping by after his last class and we're going to have a late dinner together. Riley's shepherd's pie is his favorite."

It was Caitlyn's as well. Yet something told her that even the ultimate comfort food was going to do precious little to ease her mind tonight.

"It's been three days of this, Caitlyn. Ailis and Colm are worried. They both managed to stop by this afternoon to see if I could get you to talk about what's bothering you."

"I think everyone is perfectly aware what the cause is."

Mom nodded. "Lucas Whiting."

"So why do I need to talk?"

"Because simply knowing the root of the problem isn't enough. Ailis is concerned he was cruel, that perhaps he hurt your feelings. Colm thinks you discovered his plans for the pub and you're holding out on us due to fear."

Caitlyn never ceased to be amazed by the imaginations of her family. Secrets drove them mad, which meant they would drive the secret-keeper crazy with suppositions and guesses until all was revealed. "Neither of those things is right."

"I know," Mom said.

"You do?"

Her mom nodded, the concern in her eyes almost Caitlyn's undoing. "You may have gone on that date to spy on him, but I don't think you anticipated liking him. And now you're torn. Right?"

She didn't bother to correct her mother on the reason for the date. She wasn't comfortable confessing the spying part was a lie to cover up the fact she had been sexually attracted to Lucas beyond all reason right from the get-go.

"The thing is, he really *is* the person I thought he was. He's entitled, cocky, rich, and determined to wrestle this pub out of our hands. He'll stop at nothing to get what he wants."

Caitlyn hadn't meant to lay it all on the line like that, but despite everything that happened between them, Lucas didn't pretend that his ambition to purchase this building had changed. Her family needed to know the threat was still there. Still very real.

"He won't get the pub, Caitlyn."

"It's easy to say that, Mom, but the Whitings aren't like us. They don't play fair. They fight dirty. Really dirty. And you know as well as I do, they don't lose. Name one time in the past two decades where they didn't come out on top." Caitlyn had lived in Baltimore her entire life. As such, she knew this city, and she'd seen the countless changes that had come about because of the Whitings' machinations.

As far as Caitlyn was concerned, Baltimore had lost a community center, two free health clinics, too many low-income housing buildings and more than a fair amount of the waterfront to Whiting Properties. All so they could bring in high-end condos, shopping centers, expensive restaurants and parking garages.

"And that's why we turn to people like you, Caitlyn. People who will fight for the little guy, for people like Moose."

Caitlyn was sorry she'd started this conversation. Because on top of her conflicting feelings for Lucas, she was fighting her own battle with a crooked landlord who was preying on the elderly. It seemed like everywhere she turned, some rich bastard was trying to cheat the honest man.

Pop Pop's oldest friend, Moose, had lived in the same apartment for the last eighteen years. The Winchester House was a privately owned apartment building that offered an assisted-living environment for low-income senior citizens.

Pop Pop and Moose had asked her to represent the residents who were dealing with the third rent hike in as many years. The landlord was taking advantage of them, and Caitlyn had joined forces with social services in an attempt to find a legal way to protect the senior residents.

So far, she was struggling to win that battle because the landlord was armed to the teeth with his own attorney and operating within the law, but she didn't want to admit that to her mother.

"Lucas is the big bad wolf, Mom, threatening the little guy. Which just goes to prove I'm being completely stupid."

Mom leaned back, studying Caitlyn's face a little too closely for her comfort. "Obviously he's not pure evil or you wouldn't be so down in the dumps."

"I'm not the best judge when it comes to the guys I date, Mom. My track record sucks."

"That's standard operating procedure for everyone. You kiss a lot of frogs and then, one day, voila, the prince."

"Lucas Whiting cannot be the prince."

"Why not?" Mom raised her hand to cut off Caitlyn's argument. "And no more about his determination to buy the pub. Take that out of the equation completely. If it was just you and Lucas, would you keep going out with him?"

Caitlyn had resisted considering what her mother was forcing her to think about for days. It was easy to justify her reasons for running by claiming outside forces were working against them. At least in that scenario, she could pretend she was acting on principle, taking the high road.

But that wasn't why she'd run from him, and she knew it. It was because he was a threat to her well-ordered life, to the part of her that truly believed she was self-aware and had her shit together.

Wasn't that his reason for giving her a three-day reprieve?

"Get your shit together," he'd said. At the time, she had wanted to rail at him, berate him and tell him she'd had her act together perfectly before he had swooped in and fucked it all up.

Yeah. Right. She'd been fucked up before him.

"He's...just..." Caitlyn struggled for the words to explain. "Different from the other men I've dated before."

"I know. He's a very dominant man, alpha to the core. Sammy is a marshmallow in comparison."

"How can you say that? About him being dominant? You've never even met him."

"I was at the meeting the first time he stopped by to make an offer on the pub."

"Oh. I didn't know that."

"I knew it in an instant, could hear it in his voice, in the way he held himself, always so in control. When Tris and Ewan said he'd asked you out, I was concerned."

Caitlyn rolled her eyes and sighed. "We're going to have *the talk*, aren't we?"

Mom laughed. "We had the talk when you were twelve, Caitlyn. I think this falls under the heading of something else altogether, though I haven't a clue what to call it. Should we just go for girl talk between best friends?"

"Is it going to include you talking about sex with my dad?"

"Absolutely."

"Fuck. Okay. Fine. Dad…he's…God, I can't believe I'm going to say this…he's dominant too, right?" Caitlyn had never spoken those words aloud, had never let her thoughts linger on that idea for long. It was one thing for her to acknowledge she had submissive tendencies that she had likely gotten from her mother. It was another thing entirely to think about her father commanding her mom to kneel or, Jesus, any of those other things Lucas had done with her.

"He is."

"Did you know that when you started dating him?"

Her mother nodded. "Yes. He told me the first night he asked me out."

"And did you know that you…" Caitlyn waved her hand around a few times, letting the gesture speak what she couldn't.

"I didn't realize I was a submissive. In fact, I fought him quite a bit of the way."

"Oh."

"You're older than I was when I started dating your dad. And you probably picked up on things at home without realizing what you were seeing. I mean, Will and I moved all the D/s play to the bedroom after you and Lochlan were born, but I'm certain those attributes still showed up in other ways."

"Maybe. It's just so…" she paused, aware that she was going to reveal too much with her next comment. She forged on anyway. She was messed up in the head, and she needed some of her mother's wisdom. "It's so intense. Being with him."

"But you enjoy it."

She nodded. She did. Too much. "I made that mistake before, you know. Stayed with Sammy because the sex was good. That didn't mean he was the right man for me."

"You've been so anxious to find your true love and move on to the next part. I blame your grandfather for that. Man is a sucker for a love story and I'm sure he planted plenty of seeds in your head about how amazing it is to find the one you want to spend the rest of your life with."

"But Pop Pop's not wrong. I mean, look at you and Dad. And Teagan and Sky. And well, all of you. You all found love and happiness and the perfect life. There's not a single divorce in our family, which is sort of unheard of. What if I'm the one who breaks that streak?"

"It's not a contest or a rule, Caitlyn. And you can't force love. When it's real, when it's right, you'll know it."

Caitlyn didn't want to acknowledge that she knew that. Now. Before, she'd tried to pretend that companionship with nice guys was close enough to right. She'd been so wrong. The silence between her and her mom lingered because Caitlyn wasn't sure how to respond.

Turned out she didn't need to. Her mom knew her too well.

"I can't help but wonder if your hesitance in regards to Lucas centers on the fact that he may be the right man."

Caitlyn lifted her hands in frustration. "Which brings us right back to the reason I can't go out with him. He's trying to take our family's business, our home, away from us. Family means everything in the world to me. I could never be with someone who tried to hurt mine."

"So bring him by, let us get to know him."

"Bring the fox into the henhouse."

Mom reached across the table, taking her hand and giving it a quick squeeze. "You keep alluding to the fact that we're weak, that we can't protect what's ours. While I appreciate that you're upset, I'd be careful with that kind of talk around your uncles. You'll hurt their feelings."

"I don't think our family is weak."

"And I don't think we're the reason you're avoiding Lucas Whiting. He got under your skin and it scared you. You've been struggling your entire life, trying to make the pieces of who you are fit. In one night, Lucas proved you were putting the puzzle together wrong. There are a million ways to have sex, Caitlyn, but only one way to give your heart and soul to someone who is worthy of it. Falling in love is very similar to submitting. Both require you to give up some measure of control. What you have to decide is if you're willing to do that."

Her mom always had a way of saying things that made her feel better.

"Okay." Caitlyn smiled. "That helps."

Mom rose from the booth, coming around to kiss her on the forehead. "Thank your grandfather. He always gave the best advice. Must have rubbed off a bit."

Caitlyn laughed as her mom returned to work. Then she took out her cell phone and opened her list of contacts.

Her emotions were a jumbled mess. She wasn't afraid of Lucas physically—quite the opposite—but emotionally, she was terrified. Lucas Whiting was going to break her heart. There wasn't a doubt of that in her mind. And yet she couldn't put the brakes on this runaway train. Couldn't find an ounce of self-preservation that would allow her to stop what she was about to do.

Her finger hovered over Lucas's number.

And then she realized—right or wrong—there was only one answer.

She hit dial—and was surprised to hear a phone begin ringing directly behind her.

She turned at the sound and found Lucas standing there, looking at her, though his phone was in his hands.

"You squeaked that in just under the wire." He was grinning, far too pleased with himself.

She turned her phone off and glanced at the door he'd just walked through. "You caved before I did."

He reached out a hand and she stood. And then he shocked her by hugging her. Like a genuine glad-to-see-you, friendly hug. "You're a sight for sore eyes."

She heard a groan behind and Ewan muttered, "Dammit."

She sighed. "That didn't take long." Then she turned to face Uncle Ewan. "You were saying?"

"Nothing," he mumbled.

Glancing over Ewan's shoulder, she saw her mom and Riley peek their heads out of the kitchen door. Riley gave her the thumbs-up and her mother winked.

Lucas must have spotted them too. While she'd told her mom Lucas represented the fox, she was certain he didn't feel that way.

Especially when her cousin Padraig came around the corner and caught sight of him. "Oh hell, not this guy again."

The Collins men had this very annoying arms-crossed stance they used for intimidation. It had worked on countless men who'd come to pick up her or any of her female cousins for dates.

Lucas chuckled. "There are too many of you. I was wondering if you'd care to have a drink with me, Caitlyn."

She nodded. "I'd like that."

Padraig jerked his head toward the pub. "There are a couple of empty seats at the bar."

Caitlyn shook her head. "Hell no."

"Caitlyn," Ewan started. "What about your dinner?"

She glanced down at the shepherd's pie. She hadn't taken a single bite. "Maybe you could box it up and take it upstairs for me, Paddy? I'll eat it for lunch tomorrow."

Padraig sighed when it was clear they weren't going to win. "Okay."

She picked up her coat and Lucas helped her put it on. Then she raised her hand to wave goodbye to her family. "I'll see you all later."

Ewan and Padraig were clearly unhappy with her choice of company, but neither of them sought to interfere. Mercifully, there were enough females in the family that the men had learned there were limits to how far they could push the "protector" role.

Caitlyn paused as soon as they hit the sidewalk. "A limo? Seriously?"

He turned to face her. She expected her joke to make him smile, but his face was suddenly too serious. "Same rules apply as the other night. If you get in the car, you're giving yourself to me. Completely."

"I think we should talk, Lucas."

"We're going to. Believe me. But that doesn't change the rules."

She hesitated, wondering once more about the wisdom of starting down this path. If she got in the car, she was setting herself on a course for almost certain heartache.

Then Lucas sealed her fate with his deep, demanding tone.

"Get in the car, Cait."

Chapter Seven

Lucas managed to take his first full, steady breath when Caitlyn walked toward the car. She thanked his driver as he held the door and climbed in.

Once they were seated inside, he turned to look at her. It appeared that she'd only just gotten home from work. She was dressed in business slacks, a conservative white blouse and black jacket. She was buttoned up and all business. And the professional, completely covered-up look was still sexy as hell.

Which told him exactly how screwed he was.

She pointed to the black shield between them and the driver. "Let me guess. Soundproof."

He nodded. "Completely."

She shivered slightly. "Where are we going?"

"It's a surprise."

Caitlyn nodded and glanced out the window at the traffic of the city. "About the other night, Lucas—"

"It's okay, Caitlyn. Things got intense fast. It was smart for both of us to take some time to sort it out."

"I keep waiting for this," she waved her hand between them, "this attraction to cool off."

"I hardly think one night was going to take care of that. We're sexually compatible, there's nothing wrong with that. I also enjoy your company. Usually when that happens, I invite a woman out for a second date. So…here's our second date."

"And that's all very normal, very practical. But I'm a lawyer, Lucas. I have this tendency to see the world in right and wrong. I'm having a hard time justifying continuing this, considering…"

She paused, but Lucas knew what she was thinking.

"Considering my business practices may not always be what you consider right. Philosophically, we are very different. You see right and wrong. I see winners and losers. I know what side I want to be on." He gestured to the limo. "I'm accustomed to a certain standard of living. I like nice things. And money. I won't apologize or make excuses for that."

"Even if your success means you're hurting people with less."

Lucas didn't respond. Mainly because she wouldn't like his answer. "So you're torn between sticking to your principles or—"

"Tossing all that to the wind and having sex with you again. Which makes me shallow and maybe even slutty as hell."

Lucas laughed, her admission surprising him. "I have no problem with shallow. Or slutty."

Caitlyn grinned and rolled her eyes. "I'm sure you don't. In all honesty, it's that damn cat that convinced me to get into this car."

"My cat?"

"You took in a stray—a really ugly one. It's making me think that there's something decent buried underneath the greed and arrogance."

"I'd like to reassure you that's true."

"But you won't?"

He looked out the window and admitted something that didn't come easy to him. "I think the proper response is I can't."

Caitlyn tilted her head, her forehead crinkled in confusion. "Do you believe there isn't anything decent or good inside you?"

Lucas continued to watch the buildings fly by them outside the limo. He hadn't spoken these thoughts aloud to anyone. Ever. However, since his brother's death, he'd been experiencing something he could only call a crisis of conscience.

Lucas had woken up the morning after his brother's funeral, taken a long, hard look at himself in the mirror and seen his father in the reflection. Until Toby's death, Lucas saw the world exactly as he'd described to Caitlyn. Success or failure. As long as he was the winner, he didn't care who lost.

He had destroyed countless faceless people in his quest for more money, more power. It had never bothered him until he realized the faceless people had names, family, loved ones.

When he walked into Pat's Pub for the first time, he had truly *seen* the Collins family—and it had unnerved him. In the past, he could walk into a deal, lay it down and walk out without ever feeling an ounce of remorse. That hadn't been true the day he'd spoken to Tris, Ewan and Keira. The meeting had gone exactly like every other initial buyout he'd ever proffered, but when he left, he kept seeing the two brothers and the way they partially shielded their older sister from him.

He hadn't protected Toby. Hadn't ever offered his younger brother any sense of security.

He'd jerked awake in the middle of the night on more than one occasion, worrying that he'd been as much of a threat to his brother's mental well-being as their father.

Seeing how the Collinses took care of their own had made him somewhat trigger shy, and it had taken a month before he could force himself back into the pub. He'd done better that time, watching the activity in the pub with an emotionless eye, categorizing and analyzing the place from a business standpoint as he and the architects discussed their plans. He'd managed to keep the worst of his feelings tucked away throughout the entire meeting.

And then Caitlyn walked in.

She'd agreed to go out with him. He knew that initially she'd wanted to explore her sexuality, but Caitlyn wasn't the type to hold people at bay. Even those who sought to hurt her family. So they'd sat together at dinner and she'd asked him questions no one had ever bothered to ask before because no one had ever given a shit who he was on the inside. The only thing that mattered to the people around him was what he could give them.

The silence lingered too long.

"You're wrong," she said at last.

He looked back at her, surprised. "What do you mean?"

"I don't think you're a bad person. I want to, because this whole pub buyout thing is really pissing me off. But," she reached out and grasped his hand, "you're not bad."

Lucas wasn't sure how to respond. For the first time in his life, he wanted to be worthy of someone's affections. Of *her* affections.

The limousine came to a stop, and Lucas was surprised to see they'd already arrived at their destination.

"The marina? Isn't it a bit cold for sailing?" Caitlyn asked.

"Not the way I intend to do it." He reached for her hand to help her out of the limo and kept hold of it as he led her to his yacht. Lucas was sorry it wasn't warmer, but December was determined to leave a sting this year, with lower-than-normal temperatures. While the night was clear and the moon full, the chill in the air insured no one would want to linger outside.

He helped her aboard his yacht, entertained by her muttered "holy shits" and "sweet Jesuses."

"This is insane," she said when they left the upper deck and walked downstairs. "I've never seen..." Her words faded as she walked farther into the spacious living room. The large white-leather sectional and matching ottoman dominated the room. The opposite wall contained a horseshoe bar with tall cushioned stools. Behind it was a mirrored shelf trimmed in gold that held the liquor and glasses.

"Whoa."

"Let me call the captain and tell him we're ready to go and then I'll pour you a drink."

Caitlyn was too busy walking around the room to respond, her gaze flickering from one spot to the next rapidly.

Once they were underway, Lucas walked behind the bar and gestured to the bottles. "Name your poison."

Caitlyn studied her choices briefly as she sat at the bar. "Gin and tonic."

Lucas opened the bottle of Nolet's Reserve, poured them both a glass, and then walked around the counter to claim the stool next to hers. "To second dates," he said, as they clinked their glasses together.

She glanced over her shoulder at the large windows behind the sectional. The Baltimore skyline grew smaller as they traveled farther along the Patapsco River toward the Chesapeake Bay.

"It's beautiful."

Lucas didn't bother to check out the scenery. He knew exactly what he wanted to see and it wasn't outside.

"Take your clothes off."

Her gaze flew back to his face. "Lucas—"

"You got in the car, Cait. I told you what would happen if you did."

He didn't say anything more. Instead, he watched her, letting her know he was waiting for her to obey his order.

Caitlyn put down her glass and stood. She slipped the buttons on her blouse free, slowly, seductively.

Lucas kept a tight grip on his glass because he didn't trust himself not to rip her clothes off and fuck her like a man possessed. It had been a very long three days.

When she pulled the blouse off, Lucas couldn't take it a minute longer. He covered her hands with his before she could unfasten her bra.

"What's your safe word?"

"Blue," she whispered.

He'd stocked the yacht, come prepared.

He released her hands and watched as the bra came off quickly, as did her slacks, socks and shoes.

Once she was completely naked, she glanced toward the floor, clearly unsure if she should kneel since he hadn't added that to his command.

"Put your hands behind your head."

The position lifted her breasts, pushing them out. He leaned toward her, taking one into his mouth and sucking on her nipple.

She gasped, but didn't jerk out of his grip. He repeated the action to the other breast.

"Did you like the nipple clamps?"

She nodded.

"I'd love to see these pierced."

Caitlyn shivered, her eyes drifting closed.

"Cait," he said sternly.

Her eyes flew open, her gaze on his.

"Don't close your eyes. Watch me."

He crossed the room to retrieve the bag he'd dropped off earlier in the day. She was new to all of this, and despite her belief that she and that idiot ex of hers had indulged in D/s play, it was obvious they'd done nothing of the sort.

"Ahh!" Caitlyn's shocked, excited gasp told him how much she liked the hemp he'd pulled from the bag. "Lucas—"

"Shhh. No talking, Cait. If I have a question, you'll answer it. Otherwise, you're not to speak. Do you understand?"

She nodded.

He paused, determined to hear her call him sir again. She'd spoken it to him just once, and it had merely whetted his appetite for more.

She looked at him, puzzled, when he didn't move. "I can wait all night, Cait. Do you understand?"

His repeated question clued her in to what he wanted.

"Yes, sir," she whispered.

His cock thickened, throbbed. He'd been at half-mast since picking her up at the pub. Tonight wasn't just going to test her limits. It was going to test his.

Lucas took her hand and led her to the oversized, cushioned ottoman. It was perfect for what he had in mind. "Hands and knees."

Caitlyn climbed on the large ottoman and assumed the position without hesitation. She'd enjoyed his bondage the other night, even though he'd kept it lighter, strapping only her wrists to the bed.

He was upping the ante tonight.

Pressing her legs apart, he knelt behind her, gripped her hands, and pulled them behind her back so her face was resting on the leather cushion.

Taking the hemp, he slowly wound it around her wrists before looping it higher, twisting it around her upper arms. The binding was tight enough to keep her helpless.

"Does that hurt?"

She shook her head.

Lucas froze and waited.

"No, sir. I love it." Her breathless tone would have been enough to tell him that without the confirmation.

Once her arms were completely confined, he reached for the bag once again and pulled out the anal beads and lubrication.

He ran his hand over the soft globes of her ass before removing the cap on the lube and squeezing some into her ass. She jumped slightly at the sudden chill.

"Lucas." Her voice was filled with desire, hunger. It fed his own.

He dragged the beads along her ass, letting her feel them, letting her know what was coming next.

"Please," she murmured.

Lucas pressed the first bead in. The strand contained eight, each one slightly larger than the next, with a loop on the end that would make it easy for him to remove them. He'd started with the smallest.

He pushed in the second and the third, one right after the other, and then let the remaining beads dangle between her legs. "Hold those in. Don't let them slip out."

Caitlyn's back arched, her anus puckering around the strand as she worked to obey him.

"There are five left. You're going to take them all inside for me."

"I— Yes, sir."

Lucas's chest tightened and his cock throbbed almost painfully. "That's right, Cait. Call me sir and understand what it means. Right now, right here, I'm your master."

He slid two more beads into her anus. She gasped, the larger ones stretching her tight hole.

"God," she cried out. "Oh God."

Lucas spanked her ass, two swats on each cheek that left bright pink marks. "I told you not to speak."

Spanking was never going to be a viable punishment for Caitlyn. She liked it too much. She wiggled her ass, inviting him to continue.

He was glad he was behind her where she couldn't see his face. He wasn't forced to school his emotions, to hide his smile at her reactions. He pushed the final three beads inside her ass. The last two had stretched her beyond what was probably comfortable, but she didn't cry out or ask him to stop.

There was still one more toy in the bag. Reaching in, he withdrew the small egg-shaped vibrator and its remote. Her body provided all the lube he needed to push it into her pussy with ease.

Caitlyn groaned, her body shuddering in anticipation. He left the ottoman, claiming the spot on the sectional that gave him the best view of her face.

She followed his progress with her eyes, wary, though her hair had fallen over her face partially. She hadn't expected him to leave her there, but there was no way Lucas could deny himself the treat of looking at her. His own personal work of erotic art.

He reached out to push her hair away from her eyes, determined that she watch him as well. Leaning back on the couch, he lifted the remote.

"You aren't allowed to come."

She scowled, displeased with his command. He'd felt how wet she was. How hot. Caitlyn's orgasm was close.

"If you come before I give you permission, I'll untie you, you'll suck my cock, and then I'll take you home."

Caitlyn's annoyance faded in the face of his threat, genuine determination taking root. He'd found his punishment. For his submissive, there was nothing more brutal than taking away her bondage.

"Do you understand, Cait?"

"Yes, sir." Her voice was stronger than he would have imagined, and it turned him on. She may be submissive, but she wasn't weak.

He pressed a button on the remote, keeping the toy on low.

Caitlyn shuddered and struggled to close her legs around it. Whether she was trying to hold it in or find some relief didn't matter. He'd issued his command. It was up to her to obey it.

She squirmed, fighting against the climax. Her sexy wriggling was almost his undoing.

Lucas stood briefly, unfastening his pants and letting them drop to the floor. He didn't bother to kick them off. Instead, he sat back down and took his cock in his fist, stroking it as he watched Caitlyn struggle against her bondage, against her desire to come.

It was the most beautiful thing he'd ever seen.

When he switched the remote to the next speed, Caitlyn cried out loudly, her body going stiff as she waged a war with herself.

Lucas stroked himself harder, faster, torn between yanking the vibrator out and filling her pussy himself or jerking himself off so he could come all over her. Both options were appealing.

He forced himself to slow down. Sucking in some much-needed air, he took a couple minutes to compose himself. However, he didn't give Caitlyn the same luxury.

She continued to fight against the ropes on her arms, the vibrator in her pussy, the beads in her ass. All of it was too much and she was clearly close.

Once he'd beaten down his own imminent climax, he stood and turned the remote on high.

"Come for me, Cait."

She began screaming the instant the remote's speed increased. Lucas stepped behind her as her body convulsed from the overpowering orgasm racking her.

Donning a condom, he used two fingers to draw out the still-vibrating toy, her pussy clenching greedily to keep it inside.

He pushed his dick to the hilt in one hard thrust, uncertain if Caitlyn was coming again or still coming. It didn't matter to him. She felt like heaven on his cock, tight as a vise and hot as a furnace. He pressed the vibrator against her clit to keep her orgasm going, determined to soak up every bit of the throbbing, the pounding of her inner muscles against him.

When her orgasm started to wane, he turned the vibrator off and tossed it to the couch. Then he started fucking her in earnest, taking her harder than he'd ever taken any woman.

As his own climax loomed, he tugged at the loop on the anal beads, popping them free one at a time, punctuating each one with a powerful thrust. Once the last bead was out, they were both there.

Lucas's balls constricted a second before he came, pulse after pulse of semen filling the condom.

Caitlyn's voice was hoarse from her cries and her ragged breathing.

For several moments, he remained inside her, relishing the heat of her pussy. Then he pulled out, tossed the condom in the trash can and slowly untied her.

When she was free, he dropped onto the couch and pulled her onto his lap, rubbing her shoulders, her arms, her hands.

Caitlyn didn't move as he massaged her, her head resting against his shoulder, her eyes closed.

After several minutes, she looked at him, tears forming in the corners of her eyes.

"Caitlyn."

"I didn't...I never..."

"You didn't say the safe word." Had she wanted to? Lucas's chest tightened, thinking perhaps she'd wanted him to stop.

"No," she said quickly. "All I mean is...my fantasies were never half as good as that. I didn't realize..."

Lucas released a long, relieved breath. "And you wanted us to cover all this territory in just one night."

She giggled. "Jesus. Missed the mark there, didn't I?"

"I planned for us to spend the night on the yacht. You okay with sleeping with the enemy tonight?"

Her face sobered up. He'd meant the comment as a joke, but his tone hadn't sold it.

"You don't have to be the enemy."

It was as simple and as difficult as that. He could drop the bid for the pub. They both knew it. The problem was even if he bailed out of the project, his father would most likely move forward with it. It would fall to him to protect the Collins family's interest. He just wasn't sure how to do that.

"I know," he said, hoping she would let that line of conversation die there. After everything they'd shared tonight, he didn't want to ruin the moment.

"Of course, even if the pub issue wasn't there, there are other things standing in our way."

He frowned. "What do you mean?"

"We're very different people, Lucas. Limos and yachts aren't my standard mode of transportation."

"Being different isn't a bad thing."

She considered that and then nodded slowly. "You're right. It's not."

"I want to keep seeing you."

Caitlyn bit her lower lip rather than reply.

If she demanded that he take her home again, Lucas wouldn't be held responsible for his actions. He'd let her go for three days, and it had nearly killed him. This time, he wouldn't let her escape so easily.

"Cait," he prompted when she didn't answer.

"I want to see you again too."

Her response was what he wanted, but it wasn't enough. Lucas was a greedy bastard. Old habits died hard. "No more limits," he demanded.

She gave him a sad, beautiful smile. "No more limits."

Chapter Eight

Caitlyn stood outside the door to Lucas's place, debating whether or not she should knock. It was well after eleven p.m.—way too late for a visit. She'd started to turn around twice on the drive over here, but something kept her going.

It was Christmas night, and she'd spent the entire day in a whirlwind of activity that had begun at her parents' house, unwrapping gifts with Mom, Dad and Lochlan. Then they'd driven to the pub for a huge family meal. The family was too large to comfortably fit in anyone's house, so each year they gathered at the pub, opening presents, singing carols, drinking too much Jameson, while talking and laughing until they were all hoarse.

This year's festivities had lasted until a couple hours ago, at which point Caitlyn had crawled into her own bed at home, exhausted from the day. However, she'd tossed and turned, too restless to sleep, and then she realized what was keeping her up.

Lucas.

He'd confided in her a couple of days ago that his Christmas day consisted of a quiet breakfast at his mother's house, a late lunch with his dad at the country club, and then—this was the part that had really gotten to her—he simply spent the evening at home. Alone. The whole thing sounded dreadful to her.

Lonely and depressing.

They'd only seen each other a handful of times since the night on the yacht, so it wasn't as if they were in an actual relationship, or at least, they weren't to the place where that's what they were calling it. And they certainly hadn't progressed to something serious enough to warrant an invitation to spend the holiday with her family.

God, she could imagine her uncles' faces if she'd shown up with Lucas in tow. They were only just barely holding their tongues about the fact she was still seeing the man. She had Mom and Riley to thank for the restraint on their parts. However, that control would have been sorely tested if she'd poured Lucas a glass of eggnog from Grandma Sunday's crystal punch bowl.

So far, since the night on the yacht, they'd gone out to dinner three times and lunch twice, and all five times had ended in red-hot, blow-the-roof-off-the-house sex.

Every time she saw him again, she swore she'd show some self-control. Then he'd whisper "Cait" in her ear, in that deep, demanding way, and the next thing she knew, she was naked and bent over whatever piece of furniture was at hand.

Or against whatever wall.

She blushed as she recalled Lucas taking her against the wall in the bathroom of a very ritzy French restaurant on Roland Avenue.

It was madness. And it didn't show signs of ending anytime soon. The only thing that sort of set her mind at ease was the fact Lucas seemed to be as helpless to resist her as she was him.

But sex wasn't what had driven her here tonight.

It was the idea that Lucas was alone on Christmas. She didn't like it.

She lifted her hand and knocked.

A couple minutes later, the door opened to reveal Lucas, shirtless, in lounge pants that hung off his waist just enough to give her a perfect glimpse of his six-pack chest...and rock-hard stomach.

She amended her previous reason for coming.

It was totally for sex.

"Caitlyn? What are you doing here?"

"I should have called. Or texted." For a brief moment, she panicked. What if he wasn't alone? They weren't in a committed affair, or at least, they hadn't said they were. For all she knew, he had company. "I can go," she said, taking a step away from the door.

"No." Lucas grasped her hand and pulled her inside. "I'm glad to see you. I thought you had a big day planned with your family."

"I did. I mean, I did it all. Party wrapped up a couple hours ago. I just..." She paused, uncertain how to explain her impromptu appearance. "I knew you were going to be alone most of the day and I thought maybe you'd like some company."

She held out the bag she'd brought along. A plate of dinner—turkey, lamb, mashed potatoes, stuffing, green bean casserole, Brussels sprouts, homemade rolls—and a Tupperware container with three different kinds of dessert—pumpkin pie, Christmas cookies and German chocolate cake. "Brought you some leftovers."

He frowned. "Leftovers?"

Caitlyn grinned mischievously. "Yes. It's something we middle-class people eat a lot of. It's where you take whatever was left from one meal and eat it the next day. Sort of a money-saving technique, like couponing."

He chuckled as he accepted the bag and headed toward the kitchen. "Very funny."

Lucas pulled out two plates from the cabinet and reached into the bag.

She held up her hand. "You can put one of those plates away. I couldn't eat another bite. Feel like I could pop, I'm so full."

Lucas's eyes widened when he pulled the aluminum foil from the paper plate. "No wonder. This is what you had for dinner? It's a ton of food."

"Yeah. Of course. It's pretty traditional fare. What did *you* have for dinner?"

He shrugged. "A bowl of cereal."

She was horrified. "For Christmas?"

"I wasn't really that hungry earlier. Had oysters Rockefeller with my mom for brunch, and then Dad and I had steaks at his club around three."

She crinkled her nose. "Steak for Christmas?"

"Yeah. Wagyu Gold Grade. Filet mignon. It's this thing rich people eat that costs a lot of money."

She laughed. "Smartass."

Lucas moved the food from the paper plate to a glass one and popped it in the microwave. Then he walked to the refrigerator and pulled out a bottle of Chardonnay. "Want to have a glass of wine with me?"

She nodded. "That would be great."

He poured them both a glass, and then retrieved his heated plate from the microwave before they took a seat at the kitchen table. "Your timing is perfect. I was just debating whether or not to grab a second bowl of cereal or go to bed hungry. Much prefer what you brought along. Merry Christmas, Caitlyn," he said as he lifted his glass.

"Merry Christmas," she repeated.

Lucas lifted his fork, digging into the mashed potatoes and gravy with gusto. "So how was your day?"

"It was loud and crazy. You know, the norm, anytime you get the entire Collins clan in one place. There are nearly thirty of us, so by the time the uncles have passed the Jameson around a few times and we've opened all the gifts—"

"Please tell me you don't buy gifts for all thirty people."

Caitlyn made a horrified face. "Good God, no. Can you imagine? We draw names. Then Riley comes up with what she calls 'the order.'" Caitlyn finger-quoted the last two words. "This year we opened alphabetically, which wasn't too bad for me. I was pretty close to the beginning as a C."

"You have to watch everyone open their gift?"

Caitlyn nodded. "Of course, otherwise you'd miss everything and wouldn't know what anyone got. Where's the fun in that?"

Lucas shrugged. "Seems to me, it would take forever your way."

"It does, but it's also very entertaining. Some of the gifts are silly, some sweet or sentimental, some practical. In my family, half the fun is talking over everyone else to express your opinion of each present."

He shook his head as he took a sip of wine. "Sounds exhausting. And loud."

"Maybe just because you're not used to the big family scene."

"Maybe. Did your aunt Riley make all this food? It's really good."

"No." Caitlyn reached over and snatched a Brussels sprout from his plate. "At the holidays, everyone pitches in. Riley isn't the only great cook in the family. I mean, my mom and Aunt Teagan just barely hold their own, but Aunt Lily and Aunt Lane make incredible desserts. And Aunt Lauren's homemade rolls are the bomb."

"That's a lot of aunts."

Caitlyn laughed. "Yeah. I have even more uncles though."

"That's right. Your uncle Killian has a partner, Justin, right?"

Caitlyn hesitated. Since they'd begun dating, she hadn't talked much about her family. Part of her was distrustful of Lucas's motives whenever the subject of the pub or her family came up in conversation. She was afraid he was still searching for something he could use against them. Which always made her feel like a fool for going out with him.

How could she trust Lucas in the bedroom, but not out of it? It should be all or nothing, shouldn't it? Yet, the truth was, she trusted him completely when it came to sex.

Her silence didn't go unnoticed.

"Never mind, Caitlyn. I can see you're uncomfortable talking about it."

She considered Killian's relationship with Justin and Lily, as well as her uncle Sean's with his lovers, Chad and Lauren, and realized neither triad was a secret.

"Justin and my uncle Killian are in a threesome with Lily."

Lucas smiled, and she got a sense he was touched that she was willing to share. "And your uncle Sean has the same relationship with his partners?"

She nodded. "They've all been together for years."

"I can't imagine how that would work. So your uncles are gay?"

Caitlyn laughed. "Not really. Killian and Justin are straight. Sean and Chad are bi."

"And your family is okay with all of this?"

"Of course."

Lucas gave her a funny look, clearly thinking she'd add some caveat. But there wasn't anything else to say. Her family *was* fine with it.

"I don't think my parents would be quite as understanding about something like that."

Caitlyn tilted her head. "That's a shame. What about you? Any uncles and aunts?"

"I have two uncles. My mother's brother lives in Paris with his third wife and a couple of kids I've never met. I haven't seen him in years. My dad has an older brother who's a confirmed bachelor. He's out in L.A. I ran into him at a fundraiser last summer and we had a drink together before I had to catch a flight home."

"So, that's it? That's your whole family? What about grandparents?"

"All dead."

"Oh." Caitlyn couldn't conceive of a life so devoid of relatives. "Were you older or younger than Toby?"

They hadn't talked much about his brother, and she was curious to know if they'd had a close relationship. She couldn't help but hope he'd had someone in his family he wasn't estranged from.

"Older. And I guess I should clarify, he was my half-brother. My dad's son and product of an affair he had with his secretary."

"Did they get married?"

Lucas shook his head. "No. My parents' divorce soured Dad on marriage forever. He's not good when it comes to sharing his money. He gave Toby's mom monthly child support and he made sure Toby had the benefit of his name when it came to attending private school and getting into college. I'm certain Dad intended for Toby to join the family business with us after getting his business degree. Toby had other ideas."

"Such as?"

"He wanted to be an actor."

Caitlyn winced. "Bet that went over like a lead balloon."

"You have no idea. He flunked out of college, took off for New York, but he failed to find any success. He came back to Baltimore and moved in with his mom. Dad gave him a job at Whiting Properties, a position only a step or two above the mailroom. Toby struggled with depression, started using drugs. I tried to get him into rehab, but he was determined to follow the downward spiral all the way to the bottom."

"Were you close?"

Lucas shrugged. "Not while we were growing up or when he was in New York. We'd only really started talking when he took the job at Whiting, but I'm afraid that was more boss to employee than brothers. And of course, it ended when…"

Lucas fell quiet, not bothering to say the rest. They both knew how the story ended. Despite his assertion that he and Toby weren't particularly close, Caitlyn couldn't help but get the sense that he'd cared about his younger brother.

She struggled to find something to say, something that might give him some comfort. However, she missed her opportunity.

"This cake should win awards," Lucas said after a bite of Lane's German chocolate cake. She sensed he'd grown uneasy with the direction of the conversation, so she let it go.

It was Christmas, after all, and his day sounded as if it had been dreary enough without her dredging up sad memories from the past.

"I'll let Aunt Lane know you liked it."

"She's married to Tris, right?"

Caitlyn nodded.

"That guy really doesn't like me."

She laughed. The more time she spent with him, the more she realized her first impression had been completely wrong. She'd thought him cold, serious, imposing.

Every encounter with him revealed something deeper—and better. He was funny and honest and, while his commanding presence in the bedroom sent shivers up her spine, they certainly weren't the scary, intimidating kind.

Caitlyn squeezed her legs together. Dammit. At some point, she would have to find a way to get this man out of her system. She couldn't spend more than— she glanced at the clock on his oven—thirty minutes in his presence without her mind turning instantly to sex. Of course, now that she thought about it, thirty minutes was her personal best. So she was making progress.

"Cait," Lucas murmured.

Jesus. The man was a freaking mind reader. He had to be. He always seemed to know the second her thoughts had gone south of the border.

"Yes," she whispered.

"Go into the living room and take your clothes off. Kneel by the Christmas tree and wait for me."

She stood without hesitation, tugging her sweater over her head as she walked.

Caitlyn thought she heard him chuckle—no doubt at her serious lack of patience—but she didn't turn around to confirm or admonish.

She heard him tidying up the kitchen, rinsing off his plate. He was obviously giving her time to get ready. It didn't take her long. She hadn't bothered with panties when she'd climbed out of bed and gotten dressed for this impromptu, late-night—she winced as she gave it the proper name—booty call.

Of course, it was *her* booty call, so maybe that made it better somehow. After all, she had come over here hoping the night would end exactly like this.

Caitlyn knelt by the tree, studying it as she waited for Lucas.

It was the complete opposite of the tree that currently resided in the Collins Dorm. Colm and Padraig had dragged home the Frasier fir the day after Thanksgiving. She, Lochlan and her ten cousins, along with Pop Pop, had spent the better part of a night polishing off four bottles of wine, six pizzas, and playing through three Christmas albums while trimming the thing.

It was a giant, living, green scrapbook, every single inch covered with strung popcorn, blinking colored lights and decorated with three generations' worth of homemade ornaments.

And then there were the bulbs her grandma Sunday had painted when she and Pop Pop had first moved to America from Ireland, hanging front and center. Pop Pop loved to tell the story of how they hadn't had money for a big tree or decorations. He'd found a scruffy, dying little tree someone had tossed out and dragged it into their apartment above the pub on Christmas Eve. Grandma had been so delighted, she'd grabbed a box of lightbulbs from the cabinet, painted them with beautiful wintry scenes, tied string to the end and proudly decorated their tiny tree with the four ornaments. Somehow, all four lightbulbs had survived the decades.

Although now that she thought about it, Caitlyn didn't find that too surprising. Pop Pop tended to hoard holiday treasures, considering the rest of their tree was plastered with every single homemade ornament brought home not only by his seven children, but by all twelve grandkids. The crazy, sweet part was, Pop Pop could recall who made every single ornament and when. Finn had remarked that next year they were going to have to get two trees to support Pop Pop's collection.

Lucas's tree didn't hold a single memory. Instead, it looked like something he might have ordered from some fancy department store. Something that came pre-lit, pre-decorated, pre-everything. It had simple white lights that didn't blink. Actually, white appeared to be the only color on it.

And once again, Caitlyn was glad she'd come. His Christmas had needed some good food, some color, some fun.

"Cait?"

She glanced up, surprised to find Lucas standing in front of her. How long had he been there?

She gave him a crooked grin. "Sorry."

"You really are a fan of Christmas, aren't you? Never seen anyone so mesmerized by a tree."

Caitlyn didn't correct his mistaken observation. His tree was beautiful, but it actually made her feel sad. Then she spotted the box in his hand.

Lucas noticed where her gaze had landed. "I know we both agreed it was too early in our," he paused for just a split second, but it was long enough for her to notice, "relationship to buy each other gifts."

Relationship was a nice word.

It made her feel a little bit too happy.

As much as she wanted to hold back, to protect her heart, Caitlyn always tended to fail at that. Her heart made a bad habit of falling despite her better judgment. It was a total pain in the ass, a huge flaw in her genetic makeup. And there wasn't a damn thing she could do to correct it.

"What's in the box?"

He'd looked rather serious until her question, but then his smile grew. "You're not the only one with some holiday spirit. I found these yesterday, and when I saw them..."

Her curiosity was piqued, especially when Lucas made no move to open the box.

"Stand up, Cait, and go to the window. Put your palms on it and spread your legs."

She shivered as she rose. Though they were way above the city, the building facing only water, there was something scandalous about standing in front of the floor-to-ceiling glass as if she were displaying herself for the world below.

Regardless, she did exactly as he asked, turned on beyond belief. She watched Lucas move through the reflection in the window. He placed the small gift box on the coffee table.

He hadn't donned a shirt, and it occurred to her that typically he remained more dressed during their interludes. Probably because she had confided during their third date that there was something incredibly hot about standing naked in front of a fully dressed man.

She'd have to revise that opinion. Because the truth was there was nothing hotter than Lucas without a shirt on.

He stepped behind her and, now, as always, she was overwhelmed by the difference in their sizes. His broad shoulders and thick, muscular arms—no tats— reminded her of a giant grizzly bear. His size had been one of the first things she'd noticed about him. He was imposing, impressive, arresting—and he knew it.

There was no question he could force her to do whatever he wanted. He was larger, stronger. However, he didn't use physical force. He didn't have to. All he had to do was give her a look or speak to her in that deep, rumbling voice and she bent to his will. Because it was her will too.

Lucas ran a single finger along her side. She jerked in reaction to the sudden, soft touch. It almost tickled.

"Nervous?" His tone told her he knew she was anything but.

Even so, she had just enough Collins pride in her to look at him over her shoulder with a saucy grin. "Bring it," she taunted.

Lucas's eyes narrowed. "Always trying to take the lead. You haven't learned anything yet, have you?"

He pressed a strong hand on her back, moving her toward the window until her breasts were pushed against the glass. Her nipples tightened, budded at the chill.

"Eyes to the front. And no matter what I do, don't take your hands off that glass. Do you understand?"

She nodded. "Yes, sir."

She had noticed Lucas's response whenever she called him "sir." It affected him as much as his deep-voiced commands spoke to her. She couldn't deny that, in this, they were a perfect match.

Lucas took advantage of her position, stroking his large hands over her sides, her hips, before caressing her ass. She was accustomed to stronger touches from him, so this gentleness knocked her off-kilter.

Just as she was lulled into a state of relaxation, he changed the game, spanking her left ass cheek. Hard.

She gasped, and then she groaned. She was seriously addicted to Lucas's spankings. Sammy had taken her over his lap countless times, and never—not once—did he come close to evoking the sensations Lucas did.

He pressed his chest against her back. Drawing her hair to one side, he kissed the side of her neck. She resisted the urge to close her eyes. Being able to watch what he was doing to her through their reflections was a show too hot to miss.

She nearly lifted her hand from the glass, wanting desperately to reach behind her, to tuck her hands beneath the elastic of the lounge pants and touch his cock.

Caitlyn caught herself just in time.

"Good girl," he murmured.

How did he do that? How did he know what she was thinking?

"I think you deserve a present." Lucas stepped away, and she instantly missed the heat of his body close to hers.

He opened the box directly behind her, so she couldn't see what he had, and then he used one hand to tug her away from the window, moving her until there was about a foot between her and the glass. Her hands remained in place.

Whatever he had was tiny enough for him to hold in the palm of his hand with three fingers, leaving his index finger and thumb free to pinch her nipple. He applied pressure until the breath she'd unwittingly been holding burst from her lungs loudly.

"God."

She loved the pain. Lucas had discovered that early, and he had no problem using it against her. In delicious ways.

He toyed with her nipples until they were rock hard. That was when she felt the first clamp. It was spring-loaded and tight.

"Breathe," Lucas whispered as she fought to catch her breath. Then he attached the second clamp. The sting was brief and worth it. Her body began to hum, and she felt herself slipping away from the mental, focusing instead on only the physical.

Each time she and Lucas were together, she found herself fading away for longer and longer. She'd spent the better part of an afternoon last week trying to understand what this feeling was. In truth, it felt like an out-of-body experience.

Reason gave way to emotion. Thinking gave way to touch.

In this, she was an animal. No guilt, no anxiety, no fear. She lived on instinct alone.

A slight tinkling briefly brought her back to reality. She glanced at the clamps in the window, and laughed softly when Lucas wiggled his fingers over the jingle bells attached to the clamps.

"And you thought I didn't know how to do Christmas."

Caitlyn would have laughed, but Lucas didn't give her the chance. There was one more bell.

With one hand, Lucas parted her labia, snapping the last clamp onto her clit. It was the first time he'd ever used a clamp there.

Caitlyn cried out, but the sting was short-lived, and with that final clamp, she was lost for good.

Her vision, her sense of self, went hazy.

Lucas bent her forward, running his fingers along her slit before slowly sliding two inside her. She was too wet, too ready. His fingers weren't enough.

Unfortunately, speaking was beyond her.

At some point, Lucas dropped his pants, put on a condom and then, finally, they were making the music she loved. The bells on her clamps tinkled as he took her from behind, roughly, hard, fast.

They rocked together. Caitlyn used her hands on the glass to give her purchase as she thrust back on his forward swings, adding to the intensity, the force.

When she was on the brink of coming, Lucas reached around and took off the clit clamp.

"Fuck me," she cried out, her head falling forward, dangling as the blood rushed back. Her orgasm struck like lightning and continued, rolling and roaring and racing as he removed the other two clamps and kept pumping inside her.

Caitlyn couldn't land. Couldn't find her way back. Not even when her climax had passed. She was vaguely aware of Lucas coming, of him guiding her to a quilt he'd laid on the floor by the tree, of him tossing the condom, grabbing a blanket and laying down next to her.

She had no sense of time, no clue how long she lay there lost in the blissful fog.

When she managed to rouse herself, she glanced down and noticed Callie had made her way over to them. At some point, she'd curled up in front of Caitlyn and was now purring loudly.

She reached down to pet the sweet kitten, her actions capturing Lucas's attention.

"You okay?"

Caitlyn nodded. "I am. Now. I sort of disappeared there, didn't I?"

Lucas kissed her shoulder. "I keep losing myself in you too. It's not a normal feeling for me, but I'm not going to fight it. It feels good."

"It feels incredible." She sighed, her body still felt boneless. Any movement at all felt like it would require more strength than she had.

"Spend New Year's Eve with me."

Lucas missed the mark if he'd intended his invitation to be a request. Of course, that shouldn't come as a surprise. Lucas didn't ask. It was one of the things about him that annoyed the fuck out of her as much as it charmed her right out of her pants.

"Okay," she said, not bothering to chastise him. She wanted to be with him.

"We'll spend it on my yacht."

She snuggled closer, enjoying the warmth of his body. The sleep that had eluded her earlier was definitely finding her now. "That sounds lovely."

"We'll get naked and watch the fireworks over the harbor, drink too much champagne, eat too much caviar. It'll be great."

She yawned as she nodded. "It sounds perfect."

It did. It really did.

Chapter Nine

Lucas walked into the penthouse, tossed his keys on the side table and sighed. It had been a long fucking day. Callie was there to greet him, rubbing against his legs. Bending down, he picked her up, stroking her head as she purred loudly.

"Caitlyn?" he called out.

Silence greeted him. Which meant she was working late. Again.

The penthouse sleepovers had begun shortly after New Year's with an overnight bag she refilled after work every day, but as the days passed, more and more of her things started to make their way here to stay. Now, just three weeks after the start of a brand new year, her toothbrush, makeup and hair supplies had a permanent space in the bathroom. He'd cleared out a drawer in his dresser and made room in his closet for some of her clothes. She had "her side" of the bed and he had his.

Neither of them had really discussed any of it. It had all happened naturally because no conversation had been necessary. He wanted her in his apartment and she wanted to be there. They hadn't mentioned the possibility of her moving in permanently, though Lucas had been thinking lately they should. The problem with broaching the subject was they had also appeared to decide—by some tacit agreement—not to discuss the future.

How could they? Whiting Properties was still pursuing the pub.

Lucas had been granted a brief reprieve when his father was called to L.A. a couple weeks earlier. His father's brother had passed away and, after attending the funeral, Lucas had returned home to run the business, while his dad remained in California to sort out the estate. For the last two weeks, he'd been working overtime, trying to find ways to stall the project while exploring another option for the pub. One he prayed the family would go for.

His cell rang and he dug it out of his jacket pocket, hoping it was Caitlyn. He felt foolish for missing her. After all, he'd taken her out for lunch earlier that day. Somewhere along the line, they'd established a Wednesday lunch date, and Lucas always looked forward to it.

He grimaced when he saw his dad's name on the screen. His father had expected to return to work this afternoon after a morning flight, but a storm postponed his takeoff. Lucas had been happy to have one more day away from the man.

"Hello, Dad. Back in Baltimore?"

As always, his father felt no need to waste time with niceties. "I'm at the office. What the fuck is going on with this Collins deal? Astrid tells me our offer hasn't been accepted and you've made no move toward increasing the pressure."

Astrid, his father's personal assistant, was no fan of Lucas. Lucas sometimes wondered if Astrid's aspirations with the company had taken a dangerous turn. It was clear the woman fancied herself much more important than her position implied, and he'd heard some rumors about a possible affair between the woman and his dad.

Lucas had played out the stereotypical "younger secretary marries older boss" scenario way too many times in the last year. Astrid was the last person on the planet he wanted to run Whiting Properties with if his father lost his mind somewhere down the line and decided to leave his half to her.

"I've been reevaluating the offer. I think there's another avenue we should explore in terms of the buyout, one that could prove to be much more profitable for us."

"There was nothing wrong with the original plan."

"I think you should hear me out before you decide—"

"Who is this woman you've been seeing?"

Lucas frowned. "Excuse me?"

"Astrid said you've been taking long lunches and that someone in the office saw you out with a brunette last week. I called Royce and he confirmed there's a woman living with you."

Lucas's temper spiked. "You called the doorman of my building?"

"If I want information, by God, I'll get it. No mere doorman is going to say no to me. Who is she?"

Lucas hadn't purposely set out to hide his affair with Caitlyn. However, he was in uncharted territory here. He'd never dated a woman long enough to fool around with introducing her to his parents. It wasn't like either his mom or dad gave a shit who he slept with. In all likelihood, his mom would lose interest when she realized Caitlyn wasn't rich, and his dad would warn that if it got too serious, their lawyers should start drawing up a pre-nup.

Besides, announcing that he was dating the granddaughter of Patrick Collins would only spell disaster for Lucas's plans to salvage a very bad situation.

"Her name is Caitlyn," Lucas replied vaguely as he walked to the kitchen. He opened the refrigerator for a bottle of water and grinned when he caught sight of the chicken Caitlyn had marinating. The king of takeout, Lucas had gotten spoiled by Caitlyn's home-cooked meals.

"You've never let a woman interfere with your work before, Lucas. It's time to fuck her out of your system and get your head back in the game."

Lucas wondered how his dad would reply if he made the same suggestion about Astrid. He decided to take the high road. "My work ethic is fine."

"I'm having lunch with Roderick tomorrow. Meet me in my office first thing in the morning to brief me on where we stand. You said the family lives above the pub, right? It would take very little effort to get that block rezoned to business only. It's an election year, after all."

Roderick Barnes was the chairperson of the city council, and the man was very susceptible to his father's strong-arm tactics when it came to having favors repaid.

"Why would we do that? One version of our plan has us renting out the apartments above the businesses. We'd be cutting off our nose to spite our face."

"I forgot about that." His dad fell silent for a moment, and Lucas imagined he could almost hear the wheels spinning in the old man's cruel mind. "Besides, I don't want to call in a favor with him too soon. I might need his help getting some of the permits through. I'll call Tom at the IRS. He can initiate an audit of the pub. Bound to be something there. We'll run them through the ringer."

"We don't need to do that."

"Are you saying they'll sell?"

Lucas didn't reply. Since he'd begun dating Caitlyn, he hadn't broached the subject of buying the pub again. Not with her and not with her family.

"I'll take your silence as a no. It's time to start playing hardball, Lucas. We've invested a lot of money and time into this acquisition. Failure isn't an option. We stand to lose millions of dollars. If you don't have the balls to do what needs to be done, I will. But believe me, either way, it will happen."

"Give me another week."

"For what?"

"One week, Dad."

"You're losing your touch. Whitings strike hard and fast. Remember that. Mercy is for suckers and poor people."

And with those moving words of wisdom, his dad disconnected the call.

Lucas's jaw tightened and his temper flared hot. He walked to the bedroom, stripping off his clothes along the way. Donning a pair of shorts and a T-shirt, he headed for his personal gym, intent on taking his anger out on the heavy bag.

Pulling on his boxing gloves, he spent the next forty minutes punishing the bag—and himself. He would have continued, but something caught his eye, a movement by the doorway, and he faltered mid-punch.

"Remind me never to piss you off," Caitlyn said with an amused, tired grin. "What did that poor bag ever do to you?"

Lucas tugged off the gloves and tossed them on a mat nearby. As he approached her, he saw that she didn't merely look tired, she was exhausted.

He smoothed his finger under her eye. "Dark circles."

"Rough week."

"No headway in your case?" Caitlyn had confided in him on New Year's Eve about her fight to keep her Pop Pop's friend, Moose, in the apartment where he'd lived for the past eighteen years.

She shook her head. "The lease is solid. None of those loopholes you suggested I look for."

"Damn."

The crooked landlord was trying to bilk the older tenants, nickeling and diming them with increased rents. The worst part was, he wasn't maintaining the upkeep of the apartments, and Caitlyn was afraid some of them had become dangerous for the senior citizens.

Lucas had offered some advice in regards to the lease agreements, suggested certain loopholes he'd used to his advantage before. He didn't mention, of course, that he'd employed those loopholes *against* the tenants, rather than *for* them.

He'd been touched that she had trusted his opinion enough to seek it.

She shrugged. "I'll figure something out."

He could see how much this case was getting to her. At first he thought it was because it involved someone she knew, and she didn't want to let her grandfather down. But the more he got to know Caitlyn, the more he realized this was how she approached her job. She was all-in, willing to work her ass off to help those in need.

He ran the back of his hand along her cheek. "I don't like seeing you like this."

"You could always distract me."

Lucas grinned, his cock twitching. If she kept flashing that sexy smile at him, it wouldn't take him long to pitch a tent in his loose-fitting cotton shorts. "What did you have in mind?"

"Have I ever told you how sexy you are when you're all hot and sweaty like this?"

They'd already initiated the gym—most specifically the weight bench—a week or so ago. Lucas had tied her wrists and ankles to the weight bar above her head and fucked her. Hard. While it was tempting to go in for a repeat, he preferred something different tonight.

Lucas chuckled. "I stink. You can't find that attractive. Come on. My muscles ache. How would you feel about a long soak in the tub? I have a surprise for you."

Her eyes lit up like a kid on Christmas. "A surprise?"

Lucas grasped her hand and led her to the master bath. He turned on the taps, adjusting the heat level.

Once the tub began filling, he twisted toward her, delighted to discover Caitlyn was already undressing. Weeks together hadn't dimmed the attraction or their constant need to touch, to connect on a physical level. Whatever hesitance or resistance Caitlyn had suffered from at the beginning of their relationship had completely vanished, and she approached their time together like she did her career.

She was all-in.

At least physically.

If anyone had asked him a month ago, he would have said that was enough for him. But as more time passed, he found himself craving a deeper connection. They'd mastered the art of fucking, building on her willingness to submit. Lucas constantly tested her limits, taking the time to discover what aroused her and what didn't.

At the same time, she'd come to know exactly how to turn him on too. She'd cracked his code, figured him out, and as such, all she had to do was give him a look or a touch or whisper something bratty in his ear, and the next thing he knew, she was bound to his bed or spread out naked facedown over his lap or straddling him in the back of the limo.

Once Caitlyn was naked, she sat on the end of the tub and drew her hand through the hot water. "A bath is a great idea."

Her tired voice matched his own weariness.

The phone call from his dad was still hovering in the back of his mind, eating away at his ability to focus. It was his anger that had initiated the boxing, but it was fear that kept him slamming his fists against the bag long after his hands ached and his arms were sore.

He hadn't told Caitlyn about his attempts to stop the buyout. Primarily because he knew he wouldn't be successful and he didn't want to get her hopes up for nothing.

One way or the other, he was going to have to convince her family to sell. He was running out of time.

When Caitlyn discovered Whiting Properties hadn't given up its intention to buy the pub, she'd leave.

Lucas didn't doubt that for a minute. And it terrified him.

"Lucas," she said, drawing him out of his head. He was surprised to find she'd pinned her hair on top of her head and climbed into the water. He was hypnotized by those wisps of long, dark tendrils hanging loose around her shoulders and those crystal-blue eyes. Always those piercing blue eyes.

His own personal water nymph.

He couldn't lose her.

But he wasn't certain he could keep her either.

"Are you coming in?"

He shook himself, forcing himself to concentrate. If he wasn't careful, Caitlyn would see that something was wrong. The queen of questions would emerge, and she wouldn't leave again until she'd wrung the truth out of him.

"Two seconds."

He went into the bedroom and stripped off his workout clothes. Then he grabbed the gift box containing her surprise.

When he returned, he dropped the box on a small table near the tub, turned on the jets and stepped in. Caitlyn groaned as the spray pulsated against her back. Lucas sat on the opposite end, facing her, and found his own massaging jet. "Jesus. That feels good."

They both closed their eyes for a few minutes, letting the hot water and the spray work out the kinks, help them find a way to relax.

Caitlyn recovered first. "We covered my shitty day. So why did yours suck so bad? Thought your dad's flight was delayed."

She knew he hadn't been looking forward to his father's return, and they'd actually celebrated his brief reprieve at lunch with a quick toast to bad weather.

"It was. But he's home now. Called me from the office earlier to criticize my work."

Caitlyn bit her lower lip and nodded slowly. He wondered if she'd break their vow of silence about the pub, if she'd finally ask him where the project stood now.

Part of him hoped she would.

A larger part prayed she wouldn't.

Rather than risk it, Lucas tugged her beside him, gripped one of her legs and pulled it over his, then ran his fingers along her slit, applying pressure to her clit. He could feel her resisting the touch, for just a moment.

Avoiding the issue wasn't working for her. Hell, it wasn't working for *him*. He was known for confronting problems head-on, forcing other people's hands in order to get answers.

Caitlyn was the same. He'd known it the night he met her.

Kindred spirits. Powerful souls. Stubborn fools.

They all applied.

And they were breaking character in hopes of holding on to something that couldn't be held. They'd have better luck keeping a wave on the shore.

"Caitlyn," he said, forcing her name out. It was time to come clean.

She shook her head. "No," she whispered as she moved toward him. She straddled his lap and kissed him, deeply.

Lucas was always in control, always guiding them. It was the first time she'd initiated a kiss.

He couldn't tell if her goal was distraction or comfort. He experienced both, so he figured it worked.

Lucas dipped his hand beneath the water, driving two fingers into her pussy. She gasped, her head falling back in delight. Then she dove in as well, wrapping her hand around his dick, stroking it firmly, slowly.

They played with each other for several minutes, working methodically to bring the other to the brink, to the point of no return.

He withdrew his fingers at the same time she lifted her hips and guided his cock to her opening. They moaned in unison as she sank down on him in one swift, deep drop.

Caitlyn started to move, but Lucas gripped her hips, held her still.

"No condom," he said through gritted teeth. It had taken him a second to figure out why she felt so fucking amazing. Then he realized.

"I don't need it. Do you?"

She was on the Pill. That was one of the first things that made the move from her apartment to his penthouse.

He shook his head. "No. I don't."

Caitlyn smiled, kissing him gently before sliding her soft cheek along his rough one to whisper in his ear. "Come inside me."

It was an invitation he couldn't resist. And it fired up a host of feelings he'd never experienced before.

She lifted her hips, rising and falling on him. After a month of rough, intense, fast, hard fucking, there was something surprisingly arousing about taking their time. He cupped the back of her head, drawing her lips to his. As she rocked on him, he worshiped her mouth.

Neither of them was in a hurry to reach their climax, but they didn't resist when it appeared. Lucas stroked her clit when he sensed she was close, and it pushed her over. Her pussy constricted around him and he came as well.

Caitlyn didn't seek to separate them as the impulses waned. Instead, she put her head on his shoulder and closed her eyes.

Lucas ran his hand along her side, caressing her as his mind latched onto one thought. A dangerous desire that flowed through him, taking root.

"Do you want a family someday, Caitlyn?"

She lifted her head to look at him. If his question took her by surprise, she gave no indication. Then her easy answer made him think perhaps her thoughts had traveled the same route.

"Yeah. I do. You?"

He nodded. "Yes. Very much." That answer would have been the complete opposite before meeting her, and it shook him to the core. Lucas didn't just want kids. He wanted kids with *her*.

A little girl with her stunning blue eyes. A little boy with her easy laugh.

His feelings took him unaware, though he supposed he should have expected it to be this way when he fell in love. Lucas never did anything by half measures. When he saw something he wanted, he stopped at nothing until it was his.

Caitlyn wouldn't be so easy to claim.

She turned away from him, his dick slipping out when she leaned her back against his chest. He wrapped his arms around her, his hands going to her breasts as if guided by sonar. She grinned at him over her shoulder. It wasn't unusual for her to tease him about his fascination with her tits.

Lucas squeezed them firmly a couple of times, and then he remembered the box. Releasing one breast, he reached over for it, drawing it into her line of vision.

"Your surprise."

She sat up. "I forgot about it."

"Early birthday gift."

Caitlyn twisted sideways so she could see his face. "I didn't think you knew about that."

He lifted one shoulder casually, unwilling to confess her birthdate had been listed in the file of information Whiting Properties had compiled on her family. He'd noticed it a couple of weeks earlier, when he'd been sneaking a peek at her photo. It had been written on his calendar since then. Tomorrow, she would be thirty-three years old.

Caitlyn lifted the lid of the small box...and frowned.

Not exactly the reaction he'd hoped for.

"What's wrong?"

She looked at him, her mouth opening and closing several times without producing sound.

"You don't like it?"

"How I feel about it is hardly the point, Lucas. It's...Jesus, it's too much."

Of course. He should have anticipated this, but Lucas was no stranger to giving jewelry to women. Every single time in the past, his lovers had reacted with delight. Caitlyn, ever practical, was calculating the cost.

"No. It's not." He took the box from her, pulling the diamond necklace off the silk lining.

Caitlyn raised her hand. "Put that away, Lucas. I'm not keeping it."

He ignored her. "I noticed you wear a lot of silver. This is white gold. Thought it might match what you have better."

The diamond halo pendant was only 2.5 carats and hadn't cost him more than ten thousand, so he couldn't understand her fuss.

"I can't take that from you."

He also didn't understand her refusal. "It's a birthday gift, Caitlyn."

"Fuzzy socks are a gift. A Yankee Candle. A bottle of wine. All acceptable birthday gifts. We've only been together a month or so, Lucas. That's something you'd give a woman on your fiftieth wedding anniversary."

He grinned, and then gripped her upper arm, turning her back to him once more. "Cait," he purposely used her nickname, "say thank you."

As he gave her the order, he drew the chain around her neck and fastened it. Her hand flew to the pendant once it was in place.

She was still shaking her head as she twisted to face him again, but he wasn't in the mood to hear any more of her refusals. It was her necklace and that was the end of it.

"Say it."

"Thank you," she whispered. "But—"

Lucas gripped her head and kissed her, hard. Then he rested his forehead against hers, his gaze stern. "I'm not taking it back. You can pawn it if you hate it that much, but it's yours."

"I don't hate it. It's the most beautiful necklace I've ever seen."

He smiled. "Happy birthday, Caitlyn."

She laughed. "You're a day early."

"I know. I just wasn't sure what your plans were for tomorrow. Thought maybe you'd do something with your parents."

"Actually..." She paused, and he sensed she was suddenly nervous. "Would you want to come to my apartment on Sunday to watch the playoff game with my family? We're doing fun food and there will be a birthday cake."

"Fun food?"

Caitlyn rolled her eyes. "Aunt Riley's name for appetizers. Every quarter, we pull out a different platter of food. Wings, cheese fries, jalapeno poppers, crab dip, meatballs, stuff like that."

"Damn. That sounds really good."

Lucas hadn't been back to the pub since the night he'd picked her up in the limo and whisked her away while her uncle and cousin shot daggers at him. His absence there hadn't been an accident. He knew that. It was yet another way they'd been avoiding letting the real world interfere.

They'd created this cocoon, this paradise where nothing could touch them, hurt them, drive them apart.

"It's no problem if you'd rather not deal with all of them. I know you're not used to big families, and mine is huge and loud and *My Big Fat Greek Wedding*, only Irish."

"I'd love to come."

He hadn't anticipated her response, hadn't expected her face to light up with absolute joy. "Really? Okay. That's great."

Every time he thought he'd figured Caitlyn out, she took another hard left and he was lost again. She chastised him for buying her expensive jewelry, yet looked like he had given her the moon on a platter by agreeing to spend time with her family.

There wasn't a single relationship in his past that compared to this one, which left him flying blind.

He stood up, grasping her hand to help her out of the tub. Lucas dried her off, then himself, and together they walked back to the bedroom. Neither of them spoke as they climbed onto the mattress, and for the second time that night, he made love to her.

They lay together in the aftermath for nearly thirty minutes, simply holding hands and talking about a whole lot of nothing.

"I guess I should clean up and get dinner started," she said at last.

Lucas stopped her when she headed for the bathroom. They hadn't used a condom this time either. He suspected they were a thing of the past.

"No."

She looked at him quizzically.

"Don't clean up. We're going to go to the kitchen and fix dinner together. I want to watch as my come slides down your thighs, Cait."

"Lucas," she whispered.

"I'll clean you up myself before we eat. But until then, I want to make sure you remember who you belong to."

Her breathing grew shallow, her face flushed. Both responses were normal when he gave her a command. It was a heady thing to watch her fall into sub space. She told him once it was as if the world went fuzzy and warm, everything taking on a dreamlike quality. He liked that he was the only one who could send her there.

"Do you understand?"

She nodded. "Yes, sir."

"Who do you belong to, Cait?"

"You." The response was more air than sound. "For—"

Lucas gripped her face and kissed her roughly, cutting off the rest of her response. There was no way he was going to let her finish that thought.

She wasn't his merely for now.

She was his forever.

2a2
Chapter Ten

Caitlyn appreciated the fact that Lucas hadn't let go of her hand. They'd been in her apartment less than five minutes and had covered all the introductions. The best part about this setting was that half the family was working downstairs during the game. Doing this whole "introducing the boyfriend to the fam" thing was easier in small doses.

Five minutes.

So far, so good.

Ever since he'd agreed to come with her, she had fretted over how the day would go. Which only solidified how screwed she was.

She'd almost ruined everything on her own Wednesday night. Lucas had asked her who she belonged to and she'd said him. Then she had almost added the word, "forever."

Talk about a near miss. Mercifully, Lucas had kissed her before she could spout out that insanity, along with the words, "I love you." They'd made it to the surface too many times lately. She wasn't sure how much longer she could hold them in.

Today mattered too much. Her family's approval of Lucas mattered too much.

2

"Glad Caitie finally brought you around," Pop Pop said, patting the spot on the couch next to him. "Come sit next to me, son."

Shit.

"We'll keep your young man entertained while you go get changed, Caitie," her grandfather said.

Lucas glanced at her sweater and jeans, clearly puzzled by what was wrong with what she was wearing. Caitlyn grinned and hesitated to leave.

"We won't hurt him *until* you get back," Lochlan murmured from behind her.

She turned to glare at her brother. "You won't hurt him then either."

Lochlan shrugged. "Let's just say I'm reserving that right. If he behaves, I'll behave."

Caitlyn blew out an exasperated breath and would have continued the argument, if her mom and dad hadn't walked into the apartment.

"There's my birthday girl." Dad walked over and gave her a big bear hug. She hadn't seen him since turning thirty-three on Thursday. Typically she did dinner with her parents at their house on her birthday, but this year, she'd asked to push the celebration back to game day, opting to celebrate with Lucas on his yacht instead. She flushed when images of that night flashed through her mind—ball gags, butt plugs and bondage, oh my. He'd brought all her kinky fantasies to life. It had been overwhelming. Amazing. Perfect.

"And you must be Lucas."

The two men shook hands. "Nice to meet you, Mr. Wallace."

"Call me Will."

Mom stepped next to Dad and smiled at him. "Hello again, Lucas. And before you call me Mrs. Wallace, it's Keira."

"Keira," Lucas said with a friendly smile.

Mom lifted the cake box in her hand. "Made your favorite, Caitlyn."

For a split second, Caitlyn's nerves vanished as the prospect of heaven on a platter loomed in front of her. "Spice cake with cream cheese frosting?"

"Couldn't let you get another year older without it, could I? I'm going to put this in the kitchen and see if Riley needs a hand with the fun food."

Dad grabbed a seat in the recliner.

"Will you be okay for a second?" Caitlyn asked Lucas.

"Everything is fine, *Caitie*," he teased, mimicking Pop Pop.

"He's the only one allowed to call me that," she warned him.

"That's fine. I prefer Cait anyway."

The bastard knew exactly what effect his use of her nickname would have on her. She pressed her legs together and closed her eyes briefly. "Not here. Please."

Lucas gave her a kiss on the cheek as he chuckled and from the corner of her eye, she saw no less than four heads turn to look at them.

"Be right back." She darted to her room, drawing her sweater over her head, tugging on the Ravens jersey instead. Reaching under the neckline, she pulled out the diamond necklace Lucas had given her. She hadn't taken it off since he'd put it on her. It was hands-down the most expensive thing she'd ever owned, with the exception of her car, and she was a nervous wreck she'd take it off and lose it.

She loved it more than she could say. It looked silly with her jersey, but she didn't care. It was staying on.

She returned to the living room just as Bubbles was walking through the apartment with her cousin, Darcy. She was clearly midway through some story, because all Caitlyn heard as she joined Lucas on the couch was, "But that was all back when I was a 'ho in Vegas. Back before I met Riley. Now, I..." Her voice faded as she and Darcy walked downstairs to the pub.

"Where are they going?" Caitlyn asked.

"Riley needs more barbeque sauce for the wings," Colm explained before turning back to Lochlan, discussing the upcoming game.

"Nice jersey," Lucas murmured.

"Pop Pop got it for me for Christmas four years ago. Swears the Ravens only win when I wear it."

Lucas reached out and touched the necklace. She expected him to tease her for her choice of accessory for a football jersey, but he remained quiet, looking very pleased instead.

"Just to be clear, your grandfather's nurse, Bubbles, was a 'ho in Vegas?" Lucas asked as Caitlyn laughed.

"Oh yeah. Totally."

"And she shares that openly?"

"She says it all the time. I was six the first time I realized I didn't know what a 'ho was. So I asked my parents."

"What did they say?"

"My dad said something to the effect of a 'ho is a woman with lots of boyfriends. That answer stood until I was eleven and decided I wanted clarification. I looked it up on the computer and realized my dad had done a pretty excellent job of explaining it to a kid."

"Thanks for the confirmation," Dad said from across the room, confirming Caitlyn's suspicion that at least half of the family was eavesdropping on their conversation. "I thought I'd nailed it that day."

For a few minutes, the conversation swung to politics. Lucas leaned right—which wasn't a huge surprise to her. Likewise he didn't seem shocked to discover the majority of her clan tilted left. Yet another way they were different. Initially, those differences felt like something too difficult to bridge, but now she was starting to become a true believer in opposites attract.

Her mother carried in a huge platter of wings, setting it on the coffee table. Like a pack of hungry wolves, the family descended, everyone loading up their paper plates, pouring on the ranch dressing and moving on to the trash-talking phase of the day.

The Ravens were playing the Steelers, which meant a serious rivalry in her family. Her dad and Lochlan—whom he'd won over to the Steelers side when her brother was only young, much to Pop Pop's regret—started bragging about their quarterback's stats.

The rest of the family resided firmly in the Ravens' camp. She watched as Lucas listened to them argue and chuckled with amusement as bets were placed.

"You're a Baltimore boy, Lucas. Want a piece of the action?" Colm asked, when Lucas remained quiet about his allegiances.

Lucas shrugged and shook his head. "I'm afraid I don't have a horse in this race."

Pop Pop looked at him, confusion crinkling his forehead. "What do you mean?"

"I'm a Dallas Cowboys fan."

It was the absolute worst thing he could have said.

Caitlyn cursed herself for being a fool and not questioning him about his football ties before they arrived. Like Colm, she'd assumed he was a Ravens fan.

"What self-respecting Baltimore local roots for the Cowboys?" Colm asked, aghast.

Lucas didn't appear offended by her cousin's question. "One who prefers to see his team win occasionally."

The room lit up. Caitlyn suspected a full five minutes passed as everyone spoke at the same time, loudly, as they fired statistic after statistic at Lucas. Meanwhile, he lobbed them all right back, countering with some pretty fair arguments of his own.

It ended when her mother yelled over the battle, "Cool it!"

Dad was the first to break the brief silence. "I appreciate you taking the heat off *me* for once, Lucas."

Meanwhile, Colm was still shaking his head. "Jesus, Caitlyn. It wasn't bad enough you brought a conservative into our house? You had to bring one who's a Cowboys fan?"

Caitlyn had done fairly well holding it together until that point, but Colm's far-too-serious question pushed her over the edge. She burst out into loud, uncontrollable laughter. And because the Collins clan was incapable of holding a grudge for longer than three seconds, everyone else erupted with snorts and giggles and chuckles too.

Lucas was the only one who didn't laugh, though there was definite mirth in his eyes when he leaned toward her to murmur, "There's something seriously wrong with your family."

"I know. Aren't they great?"

His grin grew wider. "Yeah. They are."

"So how does it feel to be such an old woman?" Padraig teased her.

"Careful, Paddy. You're only a few months away from the big three-o yourself."

"Ach," Pop Pop said, waving his hand. "You're only as old as you feel. As for myself, I don't feel a day over seventy-five."

Caitlyn was happy to hear that. With any luck, Pop Pop would break all the records, going down in Guinness as the oldest man ever, living until he was a hundred and twenty.

"At least the weather is decent this year for your birthday, Caitlyn. Not a blizzard in sight," Dad said.

Caitlyn rolled her eyes. "Here we go."

She, in unison with Lochlan, said, "The birthday story."

Lucas looked at her curiously. "The story?"

"Every year, our dad finds a way to work the story of our births into any conversation," Lochlan explained.

Dad didn't take any offense to their joking. "Tease if you will, but I will always be very grateful to have my baby girl. It was a scary beginning, that's for sure."

"Scary?" Lucas asked, clearly curious.

Lochlan groaned as Colm chuckled and said, "So much for dodging it this year. There's the bell to start the round. Never, Lucas, *never* ask a question about the story."

Dad ignored them. "I'm glad you asked, Lucas. You see, there was a blizzard the year Caitlyn was born, a real doozy. Keira was working in the restaurant and I had planned to pick her up after her shift because the snow was coming down so hard. Got a call from Riley to come early because Keira was having labor pains. We all thought they were those..." Her dad snapped his fingers. "What do you call them?"

"Braxton Hicks, false labor," Keira said. "Caitlyn wasn't due until Valentine's Day."

"Which would have been a totally cool birthday," Caitlyn added.

"Anyway, Riley was freaking out," Dad said. "And—"

"I was not freaking out," Riley interrupted. "I was merely concerned. And you're lucky I was." No one in Caitlyn's family ever told a story alone. Once a tale was begun, it wasn't unusual for everyone to take part in the retelling. "Called Will and then I called Lane."

"Lane's mine and Paddy's mom," Colm said to Lucas for clarification. "She's a nurse."

Lucas nodded. Caitlyn was fairly certain he knew that, but Lucas was smart enough not to repeat the same mistake he'd made the night she'd introduced him to Lochlan.

"Mercifully, Lane was here when I arrived," Dad said, taking over the story again, "because the city closed the road to the hospital."

"How did you get there?" Lucas asked.

"We didn't," Caitlyn said. "I was born right here. In this apartment. My dad and Lane delivered me."

"Not going to lie," Will said. "I was scared spitless. So many things could have gone wrong."

"But none of them did, Dad."

Mari Carr

"That's right. I was blessed with my beautiful January girl."

"You were born in this apartment?" Lucas's brow was creased.

She giggled. "Crazy, right? I actually live in the same place where I was born." Caitlyn looked around the room. "Just one of the reasons why I love this place so much."

Lucas didn't reply. Instead, he looked troubled.

Part of her, the uncharitable part, hoped he was feeling guilty for trying to take away her home. Neither of them had mentioned his interest in the pub. Not once. For weeks.

Actually, it had been long enough she hoped that meant he'd given up.

The main reason why she had wanted him to spend time with her family was so he could see what this place meant to them. It was so much more than four walls and a ceiling. Three generations of her family had lived and worked here—filling the space with a million and twelve different memories.

Caitlyn was born here. Grandma Sunday died here. Pop Pop had confided to her on her thirtieth birthday that he'd always liked the symmetry in that.

Life takes away, but it also gives back.

The football was kicked off and the game began. For the next three hours, she and Lucas shared the couch with Pop Pop, eating wings and cheese fries, drinking beer, cussing the refs, laughing at all the trash talking and having a great time. By the end of the game, Lucas was right in the midst of all the fun, tossing in a few funny barbs of his own when the Steelers lost.

But more than that, her family had warmed up to him. Colm had grabbed a beer for him during a timeout,

178

he and Lochlan had engaged in an obnoxiously long conversation about cigars, and her mom gave him the biggest slice of cake, even though it was her birthday.

Once the game was over, the crowd started to disperse. Her parents said their goodbyes and left, then most of the men headed downstairs to the pub to discuss the game with Tris at the bar. Darcy, Bubbles and Riley were in the kitchen, washing dishes, which left her and Lucas alone with Pop Pop.

"Tell me about your family, Lucas," Pop Pop said.

Lucas looked slightly uncomfortable. She wondered if that was because of who his family was, or because he realized how different his was in comparison.

"Not much to say. My parents are divorced. My brother passed away."

"Oh," Pop Pop said, his eyes filled with compassion. "I'm sorry to hear that, son."

Lucas shrugged. "We aren't a particularly close family."

"Well, then, we'll just have to adopt you into ours. Always room for one more."

Lucas chuckled as he glanced around the living room. At least four people had been forced to sit on the floor to watch the game, while her mom, Riley and Bubbles had dragged in dining room chairs for a place to sit.

"I appreciate the offer," Lucas said, though he appeared more uncomfortable than touched. Perhaps he'd reached his limit of family time. After all, she'd thrust a guy who never spent time with his family into a room with too many of hers for hours on end.

"Let me grab some clothes from my room, Lucas, and we can head home."

Lucas nodded and started to rise, but Pop Pop stopped him. "I'll keep your young man company while you're gone."

Caitlyn walked back to her room, determined to pack quickly. God only knew what kind of third degree her grandfather would put poor Lucas through. Unfortunately Darcy, who wandered into her bedroom, waylaid her.

"Nice necklace."

Caitlyn reached up to touch the diamond. No one had mentioned the expensive piece of jewelry, but she didn't doubt they'd all seen it.

"Looks expensive."

"Yeah," Caitlyn said with a sigh. "I'm pretty sure it is."

"So things between you and Lucas are serious, huh?"

Darcy had only just turned twenty-one. Caitlyn and her brother referred to Darcy as one of the baby cousins. Thirteen years spanned between the cousins, and as such, there'd been a natural divide in the older ones and the younger ones. Not that she didn't love her younger cousins just as much as the ones closer to her age. It simply meant that she, Paddy, Colm, and Ailis had grown up as friends, while babysitting the younger ones.

"I guess," Caitlyn replied, hating how uncertain her relationship with Lucas was.

"That necklace feels like something pretty serious."

"That's just it," Caitlyn said, sinking down on her bed. "Lucas is filthy rich, which means he can drop thousands on something like this and not blink twice. I'm not sure the necklace signifies much more than a simple birthday gift to him."

"Wow. I'll be sure to let him know my birthday's coming up soon."

Caitlyn laughed. "It's ten months until your birthday."

"You're right. Maybe I should point out that he missed it. I'm sure I can work the appropriate amount of guilt into it." Darcy had inherited her mom Riley's sense of humor.

Darcy pointed to the bag Caitlyn had been packing. "Heading back to his place, I see."

"Yeah."

"Mom said Lucas lives in a big swanky penthouse on the waterfront. Must beat the hell out of sharing a room with Ailis."

It was different, but not better. Sometimes when Lucas was at work and she was alone at the penthouse, she missed the noise, the constant activity of this place. She'd grown up in a crowd and didn't care for solitude and silence. Yet another way she and Lucas were unalike. She gathered he loved living alone, having his own space, the quiet.

"It's okay. For now."

"For now?" Darcy asked.

"Yeah," Caitlyn said. "I'm sort of taking things one day at a time with Lucas."

"So he still wants to buy the pub?"

Caitlyn shrugged. "We don't talk about that."

"Don't you think you should?"

Out of the mouths of babes. Caitlyn realized she and Lucas were being stupid, cowardly even. They'd let things get way out of hand, and it was past time for them to have a Come to Jesus meeting.

The problem was her heart. She was completely in love with Lucas, and not quite ready to pay the piper.

"Yeah, I should."

"But…" Darcy prodded.

"But I'm too afraid to hear his answer."

Darcy walked over and hugged her. "Maybe it won't be as bad as you think."

"Maybe it won't."

It was going to be.

She rose from the bed and finished packing as Darcy headed back to the kitchen. Grabbing the tote, she headed down the hallway to the living room. She paused a few steps from the entryway when she heard Lucas's voice.

"You know, this area is changing, becoming more upscale. Property values are going to skyrocket. Think of how much money you could get for this place."

Caitlyn's chest tightened and her blood began to boil.

She squeezed her eyes shut tightly and tried to count to ten. It was either that or run into the room and beat the shit out of Lucas Whiting.

Pop Pop chuckled. "Good Lord, son. Have you seen the size of my family? Even if we did sell for a lot of money, it would become significantly less when divided by eight. Besides, this place is home. There's no price large enough."

"Then perhaps you should consider expanding the business, take on a business partner and look into making Pat's Irish Pub a franchise."

"I'm ninety-two years old, Lucas, and retired. If I'd ever thought of doing something like that, the time to do it has come and gone. Besides, part of the charm of the pub is that it's family run and operated."

"Yeah, but—"

Caitlyn had heard enough. It was obvious Lucas hadn't given up his plans to purchase the pub. Caitlyn tossed her tote bag down, leaving it in the hallway. "You ready to go?" she asked.

Lucas stood and nodded. His expression was blank, unreadable. It annoyed her. At least, he could have the human decency to look fucking guilty. "I thought you were grabbing some clothes."

"Changed my mind. I have enough things at your place." Too many things. Things she was going to have to go back and get.

Lucas reached out and shook Pop Pop's hand. "It was nice talking to you, Patrick."

"You too, Lucas."

She walked to the door quickly, anxious to get Lucas out of the apartment, away from her grandfather. Away from her.

Lucas was quiet as he followed her downstairs. He waved goodbye to her cousins and Tris at the bar, but she kept walking. She needed to get out of here before she exploded, either with anger or into tears. She wasn't sure what was going to come out, but she couldn't let it happen in front of her family.

Once they were outside, she stopped. "I'm spending the night here."

His jaw tightened. "You heard me talking to your grandfather."

"Why did you come here tonight?"

"You invited me."

"That's right. I did. I trusted you enough, cared about you enough that I wanted you to meet my family. I wanted them to get to know you, to see that you weren't the enemy."

"You don't seriously still think I'm—"

She refused to listen to him protest her description. It was well earned. "So instead of that lame, 'you invited me' answer, why don't you tell me why you really came?"

"I don't understand what—"

"Was it to spy on us? To try to get some deep, dark family secrets from us? To find something you could use against us?"

Lucas's eyes narrowed angrily, but he didn't refute her accusations. Didn't even try to deny them.

"Were you trying to get close to Pop Pop, trying to sneak in your offer to buy the pub while the rest of us were out of earshot?"

"I didn't offer to buy the pub."

"Don't!" She raised her hand angrily. "Don't insult my intelligence."

Lucas ran his hand through his hair, looking frustrated and maybe even a little bit angry. His response enflamed her.

"I don't think you understand how many man-hours, how much money has gone into this acquisition. I've spent the better part of a year working out the details. We've bought the surrounding properties, hired architects and construction crews. You can bury your head in the sand, but this area is going to change. And very soon. That doesn't have to be a bad thing for your family. My offer is going to be fair, Caitlyn. It's going to be more than fair. You're all going to be rich. But none of you will even listen to it."

"You don't get it. I told you the first night we met. Not everyone has a bottom line. Not everything on this fucking planet can be bought and sold according to your whims."

"This isn't a whim."

"No. It's your way of life. And it sucks. Go home, Lucas. Get away from me."

"Cait." He tried to use that dark, commanding tone, but it fell short. Way short. Only making her angrier.

"Get the fuck away from my pub!"

Chapter Eleven

Three days had passed since Caitlyn had told him to leave. It had only taken an hour after driving away from her to realize he'd made the biggest mistake of his life. He'd tossed and turned every single night since then, trying to figure out how to fix things.

He was up to his neck in this deal at work. Extricating Whiting Properties, giving up on acquiring the pub, would mean a huge financial loss. The building was in the key location as far as their plans went. Without it, their other purchases were worthless. He'd spent eighteen hours at the office on Monday and another seventeen on Tuesday, and he was no closer to figuring out a way to have it all. A way to give up on the pub and still save the deal.

And unlike Caitlyn, he didn't have a family that would ever understand someone choosing love over money.

But that was what he wanted to do. Desperately.

Jesus. He'd had too much time since Toby's death to consider what his family's ambition and wealth had done to others. They'd destroyed too many lives—kicking people out of their homes and taking over more small businesses than he could count. He'd spent the last fifteen years of his life traveling down the same dark path his father had taken, living for his own selfish pleasure with no regard to others.

Caitlyn was his polar opposite. He'd watched her struggle to help those less fortunate, to keep Moose and the other senior citizens in their homes, to provide legal counsel to protect lower-income families from people like him.

She'd dedicated her talents to helping people. He used his to destroy lives so he could make a buck or two.

In just a few short weeks, she'd opened his eyes to a different life. One he didn't even know existed. He wouldn't marry a rich man's daughter, like his father did. He wouldn't let nannies raise his kids. Rather than continually taking away from people, he wanted to give something back.

And Caitlyn. He wanted her in his life. As his wife. As the mother of his children.

He rubbed his eyes wearily as the limo pulled up in front of his building. He'd left work early after a huge blowup with his father. He was running on fumes.

He thanked his driver when he opened the door, grabbed his briefcase and walked to the entrance.

"You're home early, Mr. Whiting," Royce, the doorman, said.

Lucas nodded, too tired to engage in conversation.

"Ms. Wallace beat you here. You two have something fun planned for the afternoon?"

"Ms. Wallace is here?"

Royce nodded. "Yes, sir. Arrived about half an hour ago. Hope I didn't spoil a surprise."

"No. No surprise. Thank you." Lucas forgot about his exhaustion as he picked up the pace, thanking whatever fate was at work that he'd decided to leave work early.

She was in the living room when he opened the front door, a full bag in her hands. From the look on her face, it was clear she'd intended to pack her stuff and escape while he was at work.

Caitlyn didn't seem to be faring much better than him. Her eyes were puffy, red-rimmed, dark shadows betraying her lack of sleep as well.

"You're home early," she said, her voice strangely devoid of emotion.

"You've been crying."

She turned her face away from him as she bent down to retrieve a pair of her shoes. She'd slipped them off last week after returning home from work before crawling on the couch to cuddle with him. He hadn't had the heart to move them. Or any of her stuff. He'd left everything exactly where it had been when they'd left here together on Sunday and he'd come home alone. It allowed him to believe she was still living there. That she was simply working late.

"Don't leave." The words fell out before he could call them back.

She glanced up at him again. "Please, Lucas. Don't. I just want to get my things and go. I thought you'd be at work, thought I could make this easier for us."

No part of this was easy. She knew that as well as he did.

"Don't leave," he repeated.

"The IRS is auditing the pub. Ewan's stressing out."

Lucas tried to shield his response. He knew about the audit. It was the reason he and his father had engaged in World War III this morning. Tired of waiting for him, Dad had taken up the mantle, intent on making life a living hell for the Collins family until they agreed to sell.

Her eyes flashed fire. "But of course, you know that."

Lucas would make a phone call. Call off the dogs. He was known as the more levelheaded Whiting. While his father barked, Lucas reasoned. He stood a good chance at persuading their man at the IRS to back off. But he didn't want to make a promise to Caitlyn that he might not be able to keep, so he remained silent.

"What else is coming?"

"Nothing." Lucas had demanded that his father back off, that he leave the pub acquisition to him. It had been an ugly scene, but in the end, his dad agreed. So long as Lucas had the deed to the building in his hands by the end of the week.

Two days. Two fucking days.

Caitlyn didn't appear to believe that, but like him, any fight she might have had left in her was gone. She started toward the bedroom. "I'll just grab the other bag and go. If you find anything else of mine, pitch it."

He followed her, his mind racing over what to do to keep her here. So far he was only coming up with things that would land him in jail. Kidnapping a woman, holding her hostage, tying her to his bed. Forcing her to stay against her will. Every single idea was worse than the one before.

She was standing by the bed, struggling to zip the suitcase she'd brought with her. The thing was full. She really had moved a lot of things in.

He stepped next to her, hating the way she recoiled from him.

"Let me help you," he said, pressing down on the overfull bag, fighting with the zipper. Once it was closed, he looked at her, but his gaze landed on something behind her, on the nightstand.

"You forgot the necklace."

She shook her head. "No, I didn't." She reached into the pocket of her jeans. "Before I forget…" Caitlyn held out the key to his penthouse. When Lucas didn't reach for it, she turned and put it on the nightstand next to the necklace.

"I have to go," she said after an uncomfortable silence. "Moose is getting evicted. He couldn't afford the higher rent with his pension. He'll live with his niece until we can find him another place. It's not ideal. Her place is small and she just had a baby, but it'll do for now. I promised to help with the move."

She'd lost her battle. Lost it to someone greedy and cruel. A year ago, that someone could have been him. And he wouldn't have even known about the people he'd hurt. No, worse than that, he probably wouldn't have cared.

"I was wrong, Caitlyn. Wrong to start that conversation with your grandfather and wrong to not tell you we were still trying to buy the pub. I've been wrong about everything for years. I can't live like this anymore. I don't want to. I love you."

Caitlyn squeezed her eyes closed, trying to stem the tears that fell anyway. He hated seeing her cry, hated knowing that he was the one who'd hurt her. When she opened her eyes and looked at him, he saw anger through the tears. "You can't say that to me."

"Why not? It's true."

"Dammit, Lucas. You don't get it, do you? I'm mad at you. You hurt me. And you're hurting my family."

"I know. And I'm sorry. More sorry than I can ever say. But that doesn't change the way I feel about you. I've never told a woman that I love her. I've never felt like this. I'm in love with you," he repeated.

She stared at him without speaking. Stubbornly silent. So Lucas said what they both knew. "And you're in love with me."

She didn't deny it. Instead, she said, "You're cocky and arrogant."

He grinned, nodding. "Yep."

"You're demanding, controlling."

He chuckled and leaned closer to her. "You're not really trying to pretend that's a problem, are you?"

She flushed and licked her lips. He'd become perfectly attuned to her reactions to him. Caitlyn was turned on, aroused. But not ready to give in. "You're too rich for me."

"That's not a thing."

She narrowed her eyes, but he could see the shadow of a smile emerging. "Of course it's a thing."

"Put the necklace back on, Cait. Unpack those fucking bags and stay with me. Give me a second chance. Please."

"Nothing has been resolved."

"Yet."

"Lucas—"

"Let's work through this together." Lucas could see she wasn't convinced, wasn't finished arguing, but his patience had run out. He'd been aching to hold her since he opened the door to his penthouse and seen her.

He reached out and gripped her waist, pulling her toward him. Her hands flew to his shoulders and he braced himself in case she tried to shove him away.

She didn't. Instead, she moved her hands around his neck and rested her cheek on his chest. Lucas tightened the embrace.

"I missed you," she admitted.

"I missed you too."

Lucas bent his head to hers, kissed her more roughly than he intended. Even though she was still here, he couldn't push aside the fear that she'd leave again. He couldn't let her leave.

"Take off your clothes, Cait."

She never hesitated as she slid off her slacks and panties, and then unbuttoned her blouse, shrugging that and her bra over her shoulders. It all fell to the floor in a heap. As she stripped, Lucas touched her, stroking every inch of skin as she revealed it.

Once she was naked, he lifted his chin. "Bed. Spread eagle."

She shuddered. She loved bondage, loved being tied up, helpless, at his mercy.

He pushed away the part of him that had chosen this position as a way of trapping her here. If she was bound, she couldn't run away. If she realized this was all a mistake, she'd have to stay. He had to make damn sure she never wanted to go.

Lucas shut those thoughts down as he pulled the straps on the corner posts above her head onto the mattress. He wasn't holding Caitlyn captive. He was making love to her.

He couldn't railroad her into staying with him the same way he applied force to make others give him what he wanted.

Could he?

Jesus, he was fucked up in the head.

And his stress was making its way to the surface. When he reached for her hand, she jerked it out of his grasp.

He looked at her with a confused frown. Caitlyn never fought him.

But now...

She rolled away from him to the far side of the mattress. Her grin was playful, but there was a wariness in her eyes as well. She was still questioning the wisdom of falling back into his bed.

Lucas didn't blame her. Given all the dark places his mind was going, she was probably right to exercise caution. "What are you doing?"

"Making you work for it."

Brattier words were never spoken. And they couldn't have come at a better time.

Every fear, every ounce of stress, every bad thought flew out of his head as he stood on the opposite side of the bed and let his inner Dom come out to play.

"You have two seconds to get into position, Cait."

"Or?"

He didn't answer her sassy question. He said two. He meant two.

Lucas moved quickly. Caitlyn expected a verbal response, so his sudden movement caught her unaware. He managed to leap onto the bed and grab one of her wrists before she could escape from the other side.

She yelped with surprise as he tugged her toward him. She hadn't been joking about fighting him. Caitlyn fought desperately to escape his grip, a fruitless effort.

Within seconds, he had her facedown on the mattress as he straddled her hips to hold her in place.

She still tried to push herself up, so he grasped her wrists, caging them together in one of his hands behind her back. Even then, she continued to wriggle, seeking some means of breaking free.

He tightened his grip on her wrists until she gasped and let out a small mew of pain.

"Finished?" he asked.

Caitlyn's breathing was heavy, loud, no doubt a combination of exertion and fear. She'd never tested him this way, never failed to obey his commands.

Lucas reached toward the headboard and with one hand, he unfastened a strap. With the other, he kept a firm hold on Caitlyn's wrists.

Once he had the strap, he used it to bind her wrists, and then, because he had enough material left over, he looped the rest around her elbows. It was a tight tie, and Caitlyn felt it. He recalled their first night on his yacht. He wanted to go back there. Back to the beginning, before he'd fucked everything up.

"Oh God," she whispered.

He'd heard every single tone in this woman's repertoire—from pissed off to teasing to sad to scared. His favorite was that reverent whisper that told him she was aroused beyond all control.

Lucas knelt at her side once his knot was secured. Wiping the hair out of her face, he forced her face up until their eyes met.

"I've told you from the start, Cait. I won't be topped from below."

That was the only admonishment he offered. The rest of this was going to be a test of both their wills.

Lucas rose and pulled a box from below the bed. The two of them had acquired a wide array of toys in a very short time. Actually, he'd made ninety-nine percent of the purchases. She made him insatiable. And what was worse was he wanted to do it all to her. Everything. Every twisted, kinky thing in the book.

She'd teased him once that they would be out of sexual positions by Valentine's Day if he didn't pace himself.

"From this point on, I'm going to put you in the position I want. I don't trust you to follow my orders."

Cait's face flushed, but she offered no response. She was determined to put him through his paces. Her mistake.

Grabbing the medium-size butt plug, lube and another strap, he knelt on the bed once more. Her eyes went wide. They'd experimented with the smaller plug quite a bit, but this one would be a bit more challenging.

Lucas gripped her hips and drew her ass up, her knees bent below. With her hands tied behind her, she couldn't lift her head or chest from the mattress. Time to add to her sense of helplessness.

He tied the strap around her bent knees before securing it around her waist. She squirmed, testing out the bondage. He gave her a few seconds to determine she was truly trapped, and then he spanked her ass.

He'd chosen the position on purpose, planning to rekindle memories of their night on the yacht. He hoped it would remind Caitlyn of a better time. Help her forget what an ass he'd been this past weekend.

She continued to wiggle, seeking freedom she wouldn't find until he gave it to her.

"Hold still," he admonished.

Caitlyn wanted to obey him. She really did. But everything Lucas was doing to her was too perfect, too much.

She hadn't intended to fight him when she crawled on the bed. Bondage was her favorite thing. But she had seen something in his face. Something that scared her as much as it broke her heart.

Lucas said he loved her. And she believed him. But at the same time, she understood that emotion didn't come naturally to him.

Not that she'd ever fared much better in the love category. While Lucas had protected his heart, held on to it with the tenacity of a pit bull, unwilling to let anyone in, Caitlyn had done the opposite. She'd handed her heart over countless times, tossed the sucker right into the ring, to the wrong men, always hoping that maybe—just maybe—they'd be the one.

They were both scared right now. That much was obvious. He was a stranger to love and she was an idiot for it, which meant they were on very shaky ground.

But neither of them faltered when it came to sex. It was a firm foundation. Probably not a great thing to admit to herself, but it was all they had at the moment. That, and the love, and the hope that all the rest would turn to concrete eventually as well.

Lucas had looked helpless earlier, something she'd never seen in him. He needed this moment as much as she did. Lucas needed to find his inner strength, and she wanted—oh God, please—to finally be with the one man who touched not only her body, but her heart and her mind, her very soul.

Lucas was it for her. There was no question about it.

She jerked when he squeezed the cold lube into her ass, and he spanked her again.

"Cait."

It was a quiet warning.

Holding still was an impossibility. Everything he did had her wanting to scream, to demand more, to push herself toward him rather than away.

She was thinking too much. Again.

Caitlyn closed her eyes, shut down the thoughts and let herself float and feel.

The plug he'd selected was bigger than the one they usually played with. For a brief second, she wondered if that meant Lucas finally intended to take her there, to fuck her ass.

That thought, like all the others, drifted away when he pressed the tip to her anus. She sucked in a big gulp of air and held it. It was the wrong thing to do, but she didn't have to worry about that.

Lucas never let her go too far astray. "Breathe, Cait."

She expelled loudly. At least she thought it might be loud. Her ears were ringing, the blood in her body pulsing aggressively through her veins. It was always like this—too intense, too potent.

Lucas was a patient lover. He'd proven that over and over again. Each incremental progress he made in filling her with the plug was followed be a brief retreat. He was getting her body used to the toy very slowly, letting it naturally adapt to each deeper swipe that opened her wider.

Time passed without meaning. They could've been in this bed minutes or days for all Caitlyn knew.

And then, with one last push, the thickest part of the plug penetrated her and held.

She gasped. "Oh."

Lucas punctuated the claiming with a spanking, a delicious one that wiggled the toy inside her as she cried out, begging him to take her.

How could she feel so full and so empty at the same time?

When the spanking ended, Lucas bent lower, kissing her sore ass cheeks gently, running his warm tongue over her hot flesh.

"I love you," he whispered.

Her pussy throbbed, and for a moment, she wondered if mere words could make her come.

"I love you too," she said, grateful to be able to speak the words at last.

Lucas stroked her ass one last time before rising again. She was disappointed when he left the bed, but she didn't voice it. She understood perfectly well that he would take her when he was ready and not a moment before. She also knew that until then, he would test her limits and drive her arousal to a peak a few thousand miles higher than Everest.

She was surprised when he pulled a slim vibrator from the box.

"Shit," she murmured, the curse prompting a wicked smile from her handsome lover.

Handsome. She recalled her first impression of him the night they'd met in the pub. Handsome had been just one of the words that had popped into her mind, but she'd thought the attractiveness dimmed by coldness. When had her vision of him changed? Morphed from the idea that he was a stern, intimidating asshole to a warm, funny, sexy-as-fuck man.

They said love was blind, but Caitlyn wondered if that was backwards thinking, because it appeared love had cleared her vision and allowed her to see everything she'd missed.

Lucas knelt beside her once more and pushed the vibrator into her pussy. One thrust and it was there, despite the tightness from her bound knees. While he had taken time with the plug, the same care wasn't needed with the vibrator. For one, it was thin and nothing she couldn't handle. For another, she was wet enough to float a damn cruise ship.

Lucas turned the vibrator on.

"Fuck." The word fell out the instant the small toy started. It packed a punch. She was too hungry for more, and after so long without being touched, her greedy pussy was ready to roll.

He chuckled but didn't speak, didn't admonish her. Instead, he skipped the medium speed, went straight to high, and left the bed.

Caitlyn fought her bondage, trying desperately to use the toy to find her orgasm. She recalled the last time Lucas had bound her like this. They'd been on his yacht. The difference was, that time he'd forbid her from coming, and she'd had to fight off her climax. This time she couldn't find it. Not without him. Inside her.

"Cait," Lucas said harshly. "Hold still. Or I will bind you even tighter."

She pressed her eyes closed tightly and struggled to regulate her breathing. She needed to find a way to concentrate on something other than all the stuff happening below her waist.

She wanted to come. Badly. So fucking badly.

A tear slid down her cheek. Nothing hurt, yet everything did.

Her body, her head, her heart.

She wasn't sure how much more of this she could take.

Couldn't he see? Didn't he know what he was doing to her?

She needed him. Needed him to take her, to fuck her, to claim her. To love her.

"Cait. Open your eyes."

Caitlyn shuddered when she heard his voice. The room had been quiet for what felt like hours, and while she felt alone, she never forgot he was there with her.

She lifted her lids, blinking rapidly to find focus.

He was sitting on a chair beside the bed, leaning forward with his elbows on his knees. Lucas was studying her face intently. He hadn't missed a thing. He never did.

He knew what she wanted, what she needed.

"You're so beautiful," he whispered. There was a tone of awe in his voice, and something she couldn't recognize. Sadness? Fear?

"Lucas," she started.

He stood, shaking his head. "Shhh."

Lucas untied her arms, only her arms. They fell to the mattress as she struggled to move them. He knelt behind her, his erection, still hidden inside his pants, brushed against her ass, jarring the plug, reminding her of its presence. He massaged her shoulders, kneading the tense muscles. It was bliss, but it wasn't relaxing. Her body had been boiling, now it was simmering. Either way, she was still too fucking hot, still a powder keg set to blow.

Once she had the feeling back in her arms, she used them to lift her chest upwards a bit. That was when Lucas gripped the plug and removed it from her ass.

She groaned. While he'd taken ages putting it in, he'd lost no time pulling it out. One tug and she was empty once more.

She hated it instantly.

Through everything, the vibrator had continued to beat a steady pulse against her inner muscles, keeping her on edge, but offering no way to shove her where she really wanted to go.

She heard Lucas unbuckle his belt, the zipper on his pants sliding down. She relied on her sense of hearing, too afraid to turn her head. Her emotions were tied too tightly to his right now, and she couldn't take it if she saw anything else that looked like self-doubt or unease.

Everything inside her wanted to comfort him, but she didn't know how. What was worse was, she couldn't even comfort herself.

Because as amazing as this was, there was a little voice in the back of her head telling her she was making a mistake, that she'd hopped into this bed because of hormones, not because of love or anything even close to common sense.

Nothing had been resolved. And she was a fool to be here.

Caitlyn focused on the headboard and shoved the thought away. It was easy to do when she heard the crinkling of a condom and felt more lubrication slide inside just seconds before the head of his cock touched her ass.

Lucas didn't ask permission. He didn't have to. The safe word was there.

Blue.

Never once in all their time together had she been tempted to use it. Tonight, she was.

Not because of pain or because she didn't want what he was doing to her body.

But because her heart wouldn't survive the aftermath of this.

It just wouldn't.

Lucas tightened his grip on her waist and paused. "Cait?"

Fucking mind reader. Somehow he'd sensed the change in her. At some point, she was going to ask him what her tell was. What kept giving her away?

"Please, Lucas."

Please fuck me.

Please don't hurt me.

She had no idea how he interpreted her request. All she knew was he slid inside, pressed his cock straight to the hilt.

Her knees were still bound beneath her, still strapped to her waist, holding her in an upright fetal position. However, with her arms free, she was able to rock herself.

They found their pace together, gradually building up the force and the speed. The vibrator that had been too small to help her earlier was exactly what she needed now, especially when Lucas reached around her and pinched her nipples.

She jerked roughly as she came, every part of her seizing up in one giant contraction. Lucas never stopped fucking her ass as she trembled with her orgasm. Once it subsided, he withdrew, removed the vibrator and began to unfasten her knees.

Caitlyn frowned. He hadn't come yet.

Once she was free, she fell facedown on the bed, her muscles turning to jelly.

Lucas twisted her to her back.

"You didn't come."

"I want to see your face, Caitlyn, when I make love to you."

She lifted her arms to his shoulders and parted her legs.

Lucas pulled off the condom and tossed it on the floor. He pressed his thick cock into her pussy, and she knew he had the right of it. She loved every single thing they did in bed, but her favorite times were these. When it was just the two of them, no bondage or toys or games, kissing and touching as he slowly slid in and out of her body.

For someone who'd spent a lifetime wishing for anything other than vanilla, she appreciated the irony in that. She'd finally found her perfect Dom and, while she loved the hot stuff, she preferred the vanilla.

Be careful what you wish for.

She'd had that fear at the beginning, but it certainly hadn't taken on the meaning she expected.

Lucas kissed her gently, his tongue touching hers. She ran her fingers through his hair and over his face and beard. She loved to stroke—or pet it, as she teased him.

They reached the end together. Caitlyn's legs tightened around his waist as he came inside her, filling her. She closed her eyes briefly, marveling over how two very different orgasms—one striking hard and fast, the other sliding over her like cool silk sheets on a hot summer's day—could be just as powerful.

Lucas kissed her as he withdrew, and then, because their bodies simply knew what to do, he lay beside her as she turned, pressing her back to his chest. Lucas wrapped his arm around her as he had done every night since she'd come to his bed, and they closed their eyes.

Just before Lucas drifted to sleep, he whispered, "I love you so much it hurts."

She understood that feeling perfectly.

A buzzing caused her to stir. Caitlyn glanced at the clock. They'd been asleep for nearly two hours. She rolled away from Lucas, who was still down for the count, to search out the sound.

Reaching down, Caitlyn saw Lucas's cell on the floor. It had obviously fallen out of his jacket pocket. She picked it up, intent on putting it on the nightstand, when it buzzed again and her gaze landed on the screen. It was a text from his father.

Health inspector on way to pub. It will be shut down by dinner.

Caitlyn's stomach lurched.

Since her fight with Lucas on Sunday, patrons at the bar had subjected Caitlyn to every unsavory bit of gossip about Lucas imaginable. Clearly, her friends believed she'd feel better about the split if she knew what a bastard the man was.

Judy, from the beauty shop, had spent the better part of an hour yesterday filling Caitlyn and Keira in on all the ways the Whitings had applied the heat, forcing her to sell. Countless fines from the city for all manner of so-called violations had finally left her with no choice but to cut and run. Judy insisted the same techniques had been used against Carl, the owner of the pawn shop.

Caitlyn had crawled into bed last night angrier than she'd ever been in her life, and it was what had driven her back to the penthouse to pack up her stuff. She'd walked in, determined to grab her things and cut Lucas Whiting out of her life forever...without a single backward glance.

Unfortunately, that fury had faded fast as she'd worked her way through the penthouse, looking for personal items. Every single room held a memory. And not a single one was bad.

Between the amazing sex, the shared laughter, the cooking lessons she'd started giving him, the nights they curled on the couch to watch TV, their debates over politics and sports, and countless other memories, Caitlyn found it impossible to hold on to her anger and her hate.

Lucas had told her he didn't want to be the villain on their very first date. And since then, he'd set out to show her there was so much more to him than all the bad stuff passed along in rumors. He'd proven to her that people aren't all good or all bad. Instead, everyone resided somewhere in the middle.

But now...

It was impossible to feel any of those good feelings about him. Last night, she'd been pissed. This afternoon, sad. Then confused. Then tentatively happy.

Now, she was just numb.

Caitlyn took off the necklace and returned it to the nightstand with his phone. She put her clothes back on, picked up her suitcase and turned to take one last look at Lucas, sleeping soundly.

She'd done it again.
Fallen for the wrong guy.

Chapter Twelve

Lucas stormed into Pat's Pub just before closing time. He was a man on a mission.

He'd woken up an hour earlier, dazed and disoriented. After three nights of basically zero rest, he'd slept the sleep of the dead after making love to Caitlyn.

It had taken him nearly ten minutes to figure out she wasn't in the penthouse. Once he realized that, other things became obvious. Her suitcase was gone. And the necklace was back on the nightstand.

He couldn't figure out what he'd done wrong. He'd gone to sleep happier than he'd ever been in his life, sure that things between them were on the mend.

Lucas had picked up his phone to call her, to demand answers, and that was when he saw it. The text from his father. Caitlyn's necklace had lain across the phone. Clearly she'd seen the message.

He needed to talk to her, to tell her he hadn't set up the inspection. That he hadn't even known about it.

He was halfway across the bar when Tris blocked his path.

"Get out of my way."

Tris shook his head. "No. You're not going up there."

Lucas closed his fist, ready to eviscerate Caitlyn's uncle. "You're wrong. I am."

That was when Padraig came into view. And then Ewan. And Lochlan.

Fuck. Why was there so many of them?

"It's not a good time for you to be here, Whiting," Ewan warned. Sunday, he'd been Lucas. The change in name—and distinctly unfriendly tone—was glaring. Of course, Caitlyn had confided Ewan would be the one to take the brunt of the IRS audit. He didn't blame the guy for being pissed.

He might have stood a chance if it had come to simply laying out Tris to get to the stairs, but his odds were significantly reduced now that there were four of them ready to shed blood to keep him out. "I didn't have anything to do with the inspection."

"It didn't happen," Padraig said.

Lucas suspected there was more to that story, but he wasn't sure how to ask. He didn't have to wait long. Tris answered his unspoken question.

"Caitlyn rear-ended the inspector's car."

"On purpose?" Lucas asked, fighting not to laugh.

Padraig didn't bother to hide his amusement. "Guy had only just walked into the restaurant when Caitlyn came in asking about the owner of a dark blue Subaru. Apparently it was a new car, and she'd put a pretty significant dent in the back bumper. The inspector was so upset, he left."

Lucas couldn't believe the lengths Caitlyn would go to in order to protect her family's pub. Then he looked at the four immovable mountains blocking his path, and he got it. This family took care of its own. No matter what. Brute strength wasn't going to get him through this wall.

Lucas looked around the pub. The place was empty except for one couple sitting at the bar, who appeared to be polishing off their last round. Then he faced Tris once more. "I'll pay for the damages. No, fuck that, I'll buy her a new car. I need to talk to her."

"What else is coming?" Tris asked.

Caitlyn had asked Lucas the exact same question earlier and, like a fool, he'd told her nothing. Then his father had fucked him over and sent the health inspector.

"I don't know."

Ewan rolled his eyes. "Yeah, right. Get the fuck out of this pub."

Lucas was getting tired of being kicked out. "I'm telling you the truth. I don't know what else my father has set up. But believe me, I'm going to find out." His dad's house was actually his second stop tonight. Lucas had intended to find Caitlyn, explain, apologize, and then he was heading over to his father's to put an end to all of it.

"You rich guys are all the same. You think you're above the law, think that you can grab whatever you want without consequences. Do you know how many lives your family has destroyed?" Tris asked.

Lucas had a vague idea. And it was a hell of a lot more than Tris Collins was probably thinking. "Listen, Tris—"

Tris cut him off. "You don't have a fucking clue. Judy Jenkins worked as a hairdresser for twenty-seven years, scrimping and saving all that time so she could buy her own shop one day. She finally gets her dream store, and *your* family swoops in with an offer to buy. And when she says no, you found a way to make her life hell, sending the city in to slap one violation after another on her until she was buried in fines. Cracks in the floor, chemicals in the bathroom, improper labeling. All of it was trumped-up bullshit."

Lucas had initiated that offer, but he couldn't recall Judy's face. That buyout had happened shortly after his brother's death. Lucas had spent months moving around on autopilot, going through the motions without thought or care. However, he didn't doubt that every word of Tristan's story was true because it was standard operating procedure at Whiting Properties.

Tristan was right. He'd been blindly bullying people for years. It was time to pay the piper.

"It ends here," he said at last.

Ewan narrowed his eyes. "What's that mean?"

"Do me a favor," Lucas said, not bothering to answer. "Don't tell Caitlyn I stopped by. I need to take care of some stuff first."

For four men who'd been hell-bent on blocking his path, now that he was leaving, they didn't seem to want to let him go.

"Take care of what?" Lochlan asked.

He didn't blame them for being suspicious. Lucas had been threatening their livelihood for months. And more than that, he'd hurt Caitlyn. He suspected they could forgive his actions in regards to the pub easier than the other transgression. If he had a snowball's chance in hell at winning her back, at earning her trust and that of her family, he needed to set things right. As things stood right now…he didn't deserve Caitlyn.

"It might take me a few weeks to sort through it all. I'm not going to contact Caitlyn until it's done. But I *am* coming back."

Lochlan and Padraig still looked confused. Hell, Lochlan looked like he still wanted to lay Lucas out, but Tris and Ewan seemed to understand him.

"Okay," Tris said at last. "We won't tell her you were here."

Lucas looked at Ewan. "I'll take care of the IRS thing."

Ewan's expression visibly cleared. "I'd appreciate that. Can we tell Riley to stop scrubbing the kitchen to within an inch of its life too?"

Lucas nodded. "Yeah. No one else is going to bother you. The offer is off the table." He turned, intent on leaving, but Tristan stopped him with a hand on his arm.

"Don't take too long, Lucas."

"I won't." He prayed he'd be able to do what he needed to quickly, because there was nothing he wanted more than to come back to her.

To be the man worthy of her love.

***

Lucas closed the file folder on his desk and waited patiently for his father to arrive. He'd set up this meeting for after hours, when the office would be empty, no one around to overhear them.

For the past week, Lucas had worked nonstop—day and night—gathering information on the down low. He'd had to be very careful not to reveal what he was doing. If his father found out, his plan would most likely have blown up in his face, taking down the wrong Whiting.

"Okay. I'm here." His father stood in the doorway looking extremely annoyed. "What's so fucking important that you felt the need to discuss it tonight instead of waiting until the morning?"

"I'm quitting."

Dad scowled. "What the fuck are you talking about?"

Lucas reached into the file folder and pulled out his plan for extricating himself from Whiting Properties. It was merely a sketch of what was destined to be a long, brutal breakup that would cost the company a small fortune in lawyer fees. Regardless, he was getting out.

His father walked into the room and glanced at the paper, his face growing ruddier as he scanned each line.

"You can't do this," he said at last.

"You're wrong. I can."

"Why? What is this about?"

Lucas had anticipated that question, and he'd spent countless hours considering his response. Caitlyn had been a huge part of his decision, but he knew she wasn't the only reason he was leaving. He'd started drifting away from the family business the night his phone rang and his father told him Toby was dead. Dad had said it the same way he might have said he was having a salad for lunch. Matter-of-fact. Emotionless.

Before they ended the phone call, his father had begun to bitch about how planning the funeral was going to delay work on their current project. Then he discussed scheduling a meeting with Lucas and the lawyers to go over their wills. His brother hadn't been dead more than two hours and his father had already erased him and moved on.

Lucas had lost more sleep than he cared to admit, wondering if his father would accept his death the same way. As if his dying was nothing more than an inconvenience.

But he didn't want to say all that to his father. Because he was fairly certain the man wouldn't care. Instead, he'd view it as weakness, womanish sentiment.

"I'm not comfortable with the way we do business any longer."

Dad narrowed his eyes. "Does this have anything to do with the woman you've been seeing?"

It had everything to do with Caitlyn. She'd opened his eyes to so many things. "Yes. And no."

"What does that mean?"

"It means I'm going to marry her. If she'll have me."

His dad snorted. "Of course she'll have you. You're rich. What are her family connections?"

Typical response. His father was clearly hoping to expand the family coffers through an advantageous marriage. "Her family owns Pat's Irish Pub."

The answer prompted the response he'd expected. His father slammed his fist on the table loudly. "Son of a bitch. Is that why you've been dragging your feet, fucking up this deal? Since when do you lead with your cock?"

Time to get them back on track. "We can call the lawyers tomorrow to start implementing the buyout." Lucas owned half of Whiting Properties. The only way to cleanly extricate himself from the business was to sell his part to his father.

Dad snarled. "You think leaving the company is going to protect your girlfriend and her family? Whiting Properties is going to buy that pub. With or without you."

It was Lucas's turn to smile. "No. You aren't. For one thing, buying me out won't come cheaply. It's going to take you time to recoup from that. And then, there's this." Lucas slid the folder toward his father.

His dad sat down, opened it, flipping through page after page.

In the folder, Lucas had outlined every shady deal they'd ever done. The payoffs, the bribery, the outright threats. On top of it all was a letter to the *Baltimore Sun*.

"You send that to the paper, you don't just take me down. You fall too." His father's tone was quieter, less hostile. Lucas had clearly rattled his old man.

"I don't care."

"Your girlfriend might."

Lucas knew that. He'd accepted that if he used this approach, it couldn't be a bluff. He would have to follow through. Even if it meant losing Caitlyn, even if it meant prison. "That letter and all the evidence in the file can stay right here with you. All you have to do is accept my resignation, my buyout, and leave the Collins family alone."

"You would give up the business, give up your family, all for a piece of ass?"

His dad would never get it. Ever. Lucas shook his head. He'd taken all the abuse he could stand from this man. "I'm not giving up a family. I'm gaining one."

For the first time since they'd started this conversation, Lucas saw a crack in his father's façade. "You're all I have left, Lucas."

Lucas didn't know how to respond to that. He'd never, not once in his life, ever felt as if he mattered to his dad. That had been a hard pill to swallow when he was younger. Then he'd turned thirty and realized he was his own man, that he didn't need anyone's approval or love. Jesus. He'd been a fucking fool. Just a few short weeks with Caitlyn had shown him everything he'd been missing, that he had thought he could live without.

He didn't want to be alone anymore. And though it made him feel weak and stupid, he knew his dad's approval, his love, was something he wanted.

Maybe he was more of a sadist than he thought. Because God knew that desire was definitely destined to cause pain.

They sat for several minutes, the silence and tension thick, as Lucas struggled to respond.

Finally, the answer seemed clear.

"Do you want to meet Caitlyn?"

Dad rubbed his jaw wearily. "Are you really resigning?"

"If I stayed, things would have to change around here. We'd walk the straight and narrow. We'd use our wealth to improve the city, not increase our bank accounts."

"Gentrification is—"

"No, we're not squeezing out the small businesses, not driving people out of their homes anymore."

"This is blackmail."

Lucas grimaced. "Guess I'm a chip off the old block."

His dad fell silent for several uncomfortable minutes. Then he shook his head. "No. You're not. Not at all. If you were, we wouldn't be having this conversation."

"Sorry to be such a disappointment to you."

"I'm not taking that deal. I'm not buying you out," Dad said.

Lucas started to rise angrily, but his father waved his hand and cut off his argument. "Don't look at me like that. I'm not buying you out because you're buying *me* out."

"What?"

"I want to retire before this job kills me."

It was the first time Lucas had ever heard his father mention quitting or admit that his health was poor at best. He had always figured the old guy would have a stroke or heart attack at his desk and that would be it.

"You want to retire?"

Dad nodded.

"What's Astrid think of that?" Lucas had never asked his father about his affair with his personal assistant. Mainly, because he didn't want to know the answer.

His father scowled. "I don't give a shit what she thinks. I don't answer to a woman."

And just like that, his father's inner asshole reemerged. Lucas regretted bringing up the subject. "Fine."

"But apparently you *do* answer to a woman," his dad said. "Never thought I'd see the day."

Lucas could attempt to explain his feelings for Caitlyn, could try to describe how a healthy relationship wasn't based on control or power or how much money each partner brought to the table. It was give and take, compromise. Something Lucas would have to learn—God willing—with Caitlyn's help and patience. She was going to have to have a lot of patience to deal with him.

"I'm in love with her. And for some insane reason, she loves me too. Or at least she did."

"Did?"

It figured his father would pick out the part that looked like weakness.

"Whiting Properties is seeking to destroy her family's business—through health inspections and audits—in an attempt to force them to sell. I'm Whiting Properties."

"She didn't know that from the beginning?"

"She did."

His dad tilted his head, clearly surprised by that answer. "And she still fell in love with you?"

Lucas nodded.

"You are a fool."

Dad obviously had more to say, but he wanted to draw it out. Make Lucas beg for it.

"Why?" he begrudgingly asked.

"If she fell in love with you knowing what a bastard you are, then she's still in love with you. There's no past tense. You sure you have to give up so much? Sounds to me like you've already won the girl."

"I don't want to win her. I want to deserve her."

His father leaned back in his chair. "You think you're not good enough for her? You're one of the wealthiest men on the East Coast, your family connections—"

"I'm *not* good enough for her. And it has nothing to do with money."

His father glanced at the file folder and snarled. "There's nothing wrong with the way we do business. It's efficient and gets results."

Dad would never get it. Ever. Time to press on. "Which leads us back to the buyout proposal."

"You can shred that proposal right now. I meant what I said. I'm not buying you out, Lucas. We'll set up a meeting with the lawyers tomorrow. You'll assume control of the business, while I'll remain in an advisory capacity for the next two years."

Lucas started to veto that demand, but his dad spoke over his refusal.

"I can't just walk out of here. There are too many," his father paused, "side deals that only I know about."

Lucas sighed. This was why he wanted out. It would be simpler to start with a clean slate somewhere else rather than try to wash the stains off this dirty vessel. However, there was no denying he'd played a role in creating that filth.

Walking away from it would be taking the easy way out, but it wouldn't correct the problem. Without him, Whiting Properties would still operate in the same way because it was the only way his father knew, and while he wanted to retire, it wasn't because of a crisis of conscience. Merely an old man's desire to slow down.

Dad truly didn't see the error of their ways, so it was up to Lucas to show him.

"If I stay, if I assume the mantle of control, things will be done my way." Lucas felt the need to reiterate that point. And he knew exactly what his first two orders of business would be. Not that he planned to share those with his father until the paperwork declaring him CEO of Whiting Properties was signed on the dotted line.

His dad nodded. "I understand."

Lucas was pretty sure that easy acquiescence would evaporate with the very first decision he made that his dad disagreed with. In addition to staying and assuming the mess, he'd be signing up for two years of knockdown, drag-out battles with the man.

Lucas glanced at the door. Fuck this. Maybe he'd just walk away from it all, grab Caitlyn, drag her aboard his yacht and the two of them could sail around the world for the next twenty years or so.

"You say you want to make things right, Lucas. That you want to deserve this woman." Only his father could speak the word *deserve* so derisively that it sounded like something vile. "If you're serious about that, then this is the only way to do it."

And as much as he wanted to deny that, to argue the point, his father was completely right. He had to turn the tide on this business. He was the only one who could.

"Call our lawyers tomorrow," Lucas said. "Set up the meeting."

Dad rose and started to walk out. Lucas was used to abrupt goodbyes. It appeared this one would be no different.

"This woman," his dad said, stopping at the doorway.

"Yes?"

"She better be worth all this."

Lucas smiled. Of everything that had been discussed in this office the past few minutes, that was the only thing Lucas was sure of, that he knew was right.

"She is."

Chapter Thirteen

Caitlyn walked into Pat's Pub with Colm, covering her mouth as she yawned. It had been a long day at the end of a long week at the end of a long month. She'd walked away from Lucas Whiting four weeks, three days and seventeen hours ago. Not that she was counting.

And in that time, she had done two things. Worked herself into exhaustion, then come home to cry herself to sleep. Tonight probably wouldn't be any different, though she was determined to try. She couldn't keep walking this path. It was time to shed the woe-is-me routine and move on. Somehow.

Ailis had texted her just before she'd left the office, claiming she had a surprise for her when she got home. Caitlyn had resisted the urge to text back, begging her cousin to postpone whatever she had planned. If she was going to start fresh, she needed to at least start. Tonight was as good a time as any.

Her family had rallied around her, supporting her as she struggled to recover from yet another heartbreak. Each and every one of them had the right to say, "I told you so." Not a single one of them had.

They'd comforted her, kept her company, tried to cheer her up. Her mom and Riley had fed her all her favorite foods. Uncle Tris always greeted her upon her return home with an ice-cold Guinness and a joke. Uncle Ewan was the king of hugs. Somehow he could always take one look at her and know if she needed one of his warm, wonderful bear hugs.

The hardest part about the whole breakup was trying to hide her depression from Pop Pop. No one had told him about the threat to the pub—one that appeared to have disappeared as completely as Lucas—so she'd tried to keep her answers to his questions vague. He knew she and Lucas had broken up and that it was something that couldn't be fixed and that she was devastated.

And because it was Pop Pop, and because he was the most wonderful man in the world, he'd let her cry on his shoulder countless times, all while promising her there was someone out there waiting to love her forever.

Every time he said it, she saw Lucas's face and cried harder.

"I'm going straight up," she said to Colm.

"What about Ailis's surprise?"

Caitlyn shook her head. "I don't have the energy for it."

Colm pointed toward the bar. "I think you're going to have to summon some up."

Caitlyn followed the direction of his finger, her brain struggling to process what her eyes were seeing.

Lucas was sitting between Pop Pop and her dad at the bar. He was drinking a Guinness and they were all laughing at something Tris had just said.

The entire scene was too friendly, too nice. Too confusing.

Apparently her presence had just been noticed. Padraig looked like a mirror reflection of his twin,

Colm, both of them pointing in opposite directions, toward each other.

Lucas swiveled on the stool, his smile still there, though the pleasure that had been on his face seconds before had hardened to something else. Not nervousness. Determination.

Oh shit.

She'd seen that look before.

Typically two seconds before she took off her clothes and knelt in front of him.

She shook her head, though no one had said a word. "No. No. Absolutely not."

Caitlyn started to back up, but was surprised to feel Colm's hand against her back, holding her in place. Since when had everyone switched over to Team Lucas?

She flashed her cousin an angry look. "What's going on?"

"I think you should talk to him."

"I don't want to."

Colm smiled and gave her a quick kiss on the cheek, the show of affection completely out of character. "You're not a coward, Caitlyn, so stop acting like one."

Fucker. He knew how to tweak her pride perfectly.

"Caitlyn."

She turned, feeling ridiculously relieved that Lucas hadn't called her Cait. "Lucas," she replied coldly.

"Can we talk?"

It had been radio silence from the man since she'd walked out of his apartment. Not a single email, text, call.

Nothing. No "why did you leave?" No "I'm sorry." No "Good riddance." No "fuck you."

Nothing. Just silence.

Of course, she'd sort of started the whole thing when she left while he was sleeping. She shoved that thought away, refusing to feel guilty. This wasn't about her. It was about him being a big, fat jerk.

"You left it a little too late, Lucas. It's been a month. I've moved on."

Liar, liar, pants on fire.

Colm snickered, revealing her lie.

She shot him a dirty look. "Don't help me, Colm."

"Go talk to the guy."

What the fuck was going on here?

She started to pick a fight with her cousin. It was easier to lash out at him. He was family, after all, which meant he'd have to forgive her.

Lucas stopped her when he reached out and took her hand.

She tried to tug it away, but he held tight. "Please, Cait."

Caitlyn squeezed her eyes closed, determined she wouldn't cry. "Don't call me that."

Lucas stepped closer, clearly seeing the tears she was fighting. He wrapped one arm around her waist and whispered in her ear, "You're always going to be my Cait."

She shook her head. "Why are you here?"

"Come sit with me?"

Colm had suggested she summon some energy, but she couldn't. She'd been numb for weeks and that feeling wasn't going away.

She let him lead her to a table near the back. The same table they'd shared the night they met, and she had foolishly agreed to go out on a date with him.

"I need to say I'm sorry first," Lucas began as soon as they sat down.

"Okay." Caitlyn switched into autopilot. If she could just keep her answers short and simple, maybe she could make it through this relatively unscathed.

Yeah. Right.

"I actually showed up here the night you left."

She frowned. He had?

"I asked your uncles and the others not to tell you."

Caitlyn glanced toward the bar. Every family member had been looking at them, but the second she turned her gaze, they quickly looked away, trying to act casual. She would have laughed if she weren't so annoyed.

"I can figure out what uncles, but which others? I want to know who to kill later."

Lucas chuckled, mistaking her question for a joke. It wasn't.

"I'm sorry it took me so long to come see you. It's just…I've been really busy. A week after you left, I took over Whiting Properties. My father has stepped down as CEO, and while he remains as a consultant, his role will slowly diminish and in two years, he's retiring from the business completely."

If he thought that tidbit was going to make her feel better, he'd missed the mark by a mile.

"Congratulations. I guess."

He forged on. "Whiting Properties is no longer interested in acquiring Pat's Pub."

No wonder her family was being so chummy. Lucas had just set them free.

"Really?" She failed to hide the skepticism in her voice.

He grasped her hand, leaning toward her. "Really. Our plans for this neighborhood have changed. Part of the charm of our city is its older streets with small, family-run businesses."

She rolled her eyes. "Is that right?"

"Yeah. I'm getting sick of driving by chain restaurants and high-end department stores. Part of the reason I noticed Pat's Pub to begin with was because it was unique and different and inviting."

"So naturally, you thought you'd swoop in, buy it, wipe all that away with a bulldozer and make it look exactly like the crap you hate."

"Naturally," he replied, taking her sarcasm and turning it into a joke. "In truth, it all came down to an issue of time and funds. I've decided to invest my money elsewhere."

"Oh?"

"Yeah. I bought this apartment complex on Fairmont Street."

Caitlyn's stomach lurched. "Moose's building?"

"I've brought in some architects who are redesigning the place, updating it and making it safer."

"Safer for what?" she asked.

"Senior citizens, like Moose."

Caitlyn felt like she was slogging in mud, trying to keep up with Lucas. Every word he said kept knocking her back a few steps. "Moose can't afford a fancy—"

"The rent's not going to be expensive. I've talked to the head of social services. We're setting it up right.

It'll be affordable housing for low-income senior citizens who are still able to live on their own without assisted care."

Caitlyn had managed to stem her brokenhearted tears, but she didn't bother to hide these. He'd done what she couldn't. He had saved Moose's home.

"Lucas," she whispered.

"I'm calling it the Collins House. I was hoping you would serve on the committee overseeing the renovations."

She was overwhelmed. Touched beyond belief. "You didn't have to do all of this. I mean—"

"I did. God, Caitlyn. I did. I've spent the first half of my life living for just me. I've hurt so many people, including you and your family. I didn't even realize there was another way to be until I met you."

"Lucas, you were a good man when I met you. It was just sort of buried underneath…"

"A cocky asshole?"

She giggled. "Just a little one."

"Your memory sucks."

Caitlyn sobered up when she considered what he must have gone through in the last month to make so many changes. "How did your dad take all of this?"

Lucas shrugged. "Let's just say it's going to be a long two years."

"He's angry?"

"My dad has been angry pretty much every day of his life. I can deal with that. He's struggling with the new me."

"Struggling sounds more promising than dismissing."

Lucas nodded. "I agree. He wants to meet you."

"Shit," she murmured.

Lucas laughed loudly, the noise drawing Caitlyn's attention to the restaurant side of the pub. She'd been so focused on Lucas she hadn't noticed her mom, Riley and Ewan all hovering near the opening. Unlike the yahoos at the bar, none of them pretended they weren't staring when she glanced their way.

Instead, Ewan and her mom smiled, while Riley blew her a kiss.

Lucas lifted her hand and kissed her palm. "You should be grateful it's just my dad. Meanwhile, it appears someone has thrown up the Collins Bat Signal. They keep rolling in."

Caitlyn glanced around the pub and groaned. Lucas wasn't exaggerating. At some point, Finn and his dad, Aaron, had arrived with Bubbles. That was probably Riley's doing. Her brother, Lochlan, had joined their dad at the bar. Ailis, Sunnie and Yvonne were standing near the stage, pretending to chat with Hunter during his break. She might have believed they weren't discussing her if they didn't all keep looking over and then quickly glancing away.

"Sorry," she muttered. "I'd call them off if I could, but they're a force of nature. I'd have better luck taming a tornado."

"I like that they're so protective of you."

She was too.

"But now it's my turn. Move in with me."

"You can't make a leap like that. I haven't even had time to process the fact that I'm not still equal parts sad and pissed off yet."

"You're not?"

Caitlyn shook her head. "No. I'm not. But that doesn't change the fact that we haven't spoken in weeks. I thought we were done forever."

Lucas clearly didn't agree. "I never thought that. Not for one second. I wasn't going to rest until I got you back, and I'm not spending another night without you in my bed, Caitlyn. I hate it. And Callie misses you."

"Dirty pool, using the cat against me. You know I love her."

"And I love you." He reached into his pocket and pulled out her necklace. "This is the last time I'm putting this back on you, Cait."

Her pussy clenched. Damn him.

She twisted in her chair and lifted her hair as he fastened the clasp. She looked down and touched the diamond, struggling to believe this was all really happening. Her life had been completely upended in the space of ten short minutes.

Apparently the return of her necklace had released some invisible chains on her family.

Her dad was the first to arrive at the table. "Didn't have a chance to say hello when you got here, Caitlyn."

She laughed at her dad's weak opening, especially when she knew how worried he had been about her. He'd texted her every single night the past month to share some inspirational quote or line of poetry and to tell her he loved her. "I'm good, Dad, but that doesn't mean you shouldn't keep texting me every night. I sort of look forward to it."

Dad chuckled. "I'll keep texting. And I'm glad everything is settled." And then, because he was her dad and protective as hell, he turned his attention to Lucas. "I don't like to see my daughter cry."

"Dad," she warned, but Lucas shook his head.

"No, Caitlyn. I understand I have some making up to do, but I promise you, I won't hurt her again."

Dad sized up Lucas, studying him for a few moments before his expression cleared. "Good."

Her mom walked over next, smiling widely. "Everything okay now?"

Caitlyn nodded. "Yeah."

Lucas tugged her chair next to his, wrapping his arm around her shoulders. "She's moving in with me."

Caitlyn narrowed her eyes. "I didn't say yes to that, Lucas."

Before Lucas could continue the argument, Ailis and Sunnie were there as well, and they'd overheard Lucas's proclamation. "Oh, Caitlyn, that's great! We'll help you pack."

"I just said—"

"Did Lucas tell you the offer for the pub is off the table?" Ailis asked.

Caitlyn nodded.

"And about the Collins House?" Sunnie added.

Again, she nodded.

Sunnie and Ailis looked at each other and rolled their eyes. "She's totally moving in with him," Sunnie said to Ailis, cutting Caitlyn out of the conversation completely.

"Yep," Ailis agreed. "We're going to run upstairs and get started on the packing."

"Why do I get the feeling this is less about me and my boyfriend getting back together and more about Ailis wanting her own room?" Caitlyn called out to her cousins' retreating forms as they dashed upstairs.

"Boyfriend, huh?" Lucas teased.

"Shut up."

"I'm very happy for both of you," Mom said, laughing, as she and Dad walked back to the restaurant.

Lucas cupped the back of her neck, turning her face to his. Their lips were a mere inch apart, and Caitlyn could smell the soft scent of Irish beer on his breath. "Do we have to stick around for everyone's stamp of approval?"

She closed her eyes, her body responding to his nearness, the firm grip of his hand on her neck.

"Please tell me you brought the limo," she murmured.

He grinned. "I love you."

They stood up, intent on leaving, but there was one last person she needed to talk to first.

Lucas followed her lead when she swung them by the bar. Tris and Padraig were standing behind the counter, discussing the latest hockey game with Lochlan and Pop Pop.

"Hey, Pop Pop. Lucas and I are going to head out for a little while." Her grandfather was well aware of the fact she'd spent most of January living at Lucas's apartment, but that didn't mean she was going to blatantly admit to heading out for the night for a hookup.

Pop Pop looked at her and then at Lucas. "I see that. Looks like true love won this round."

Caitlyn bent forward and kissed her grandfather on the cheek. "Always the romantic," she murmured in his ear.

"It's the only way to live, Caitie-bug. I'm glad to see a smile on this pretty face again, my girl. Now go on. Go have some fun with your young man."

Lucas shook Pop Pop's hands and then Tristan's. Caitlyn suspected she'd missed a couple conversations somewhere, but for now, she was too happy to care.

She and Lucas walked out and she hugged him when she saw the limo waiting by the curb. The driver hadn't been there when she got home, or she would have walked in the opposite direction of the pub and holed up in a hotel for the night. No doubt Lucas had foreseen that and told the poor driver to hide the car.

Once they were ensconced in the back of the limo, Lucas took her in his arms and gave her the kiss she'd dreamed of every night they'd been apart.

"Want you," she murmured against his lips.

"I'm yours. For as long as you'll have me."

"Forever. I'll have you forever."

Lucas reached for the hem of her skirt and lifted it to her waist. "I can't do this with finesse or patience, Caitlyn."

"Don't want either." She fumbled with the fastening to his belt and pants.

He groaned when she reached inside and gripped his hard cock.

"Straddle my thighs. Ride me, Cait."

If she had thought for one second being on top would give her some sort of power, Lucas corrected that misunderstanding in an instant.

Gripping her hips, he lifted her as she placed the head of his dick at her opening. That was as much control as she had.

Lucas pulled her down roughly until he was seated to hilt. He took her deep and hard, using those muscular arms of his to drive the speed. All Caitlyn could do was hold on for the ride.

Her orgasm hit within a matter of minutes, shaking her to the core. She was grateful for the soundproof glass between them and the driver. She wasn't sure, but she thought she might have screamed.

When she pulled herself back to the present, her head was resting on Lucas's shoulder.

"Ready for more?"

She only had time to nod once. Then Lucas lifted her slightly, pressing her to her back on the seat. He pounded inside her like a man possessed, and she realized just how hard the past few weeks had been on him.

"Harder," she urged him. "I'm yours, Lucas. God. I'm yours. Take me."

He reached for her hair, pulling it until her scalp stung, as he lifted her face to his. "I'm never letting you go again."

"Thought. Never. Was a. Dangerous. Word," she gasped, as he continued to thrust inside. She'd be sore tomorrow. She didn't care.

"Never," he repeated, more forcefully than before. She had hurt him when she left. For weeks, she'd thought of nothing but *her* broken heart. Caitlyn had never considered Lucas's suffering as well.

"Never," she promised. "Never leaving."

He stroked her clit and her back arched as she came again, and this time, Lucas was with her. He came inside her, filling her. She had missed this. Missed him.

For several minutes, they fought to catch their breath. Lucas remained on top of her, inside her.

"Babies. I want babies with you."

She grinned. "It's a marathon, Lucas. Not a sprint. We haven't been back together an hour and you've already moved me in and demanded babies."

He didn't bother to look chagrined. "This would all be a lot easier if you'd just say yes."

"I'm sure it would be. For you."

"Cait." He purposely deepened his voice.

"Oh, you silly man. Did you really think that would work?"

He shrugged. "It works in bed."

"That's right. In bed."

"Will you consider moving in with me? And having my baby?"

She lifted her head and kissed him on the cheek. "Wow. Those were actual requests, not demands. Progress, Mr. Whiting."

"While we're on the subject of names, how do you feel about Mrs. Whiting?"

Caitlyn sighed exaggeratedly. "So much for slowing down."

"I can go slow," Lucas said as he lifted his hips, then pushed back inside her very, very slowly.

"I'd be impressed with the pace if I weren't so overwhelmed by how freaking fast that recovery was."

Lucas laughed. "Cait?"

"Hmmm."

"Shut up."

They laughed. And then they moaned. And then they lay together in the aftermath and dreamed about the future.

Mari Carr

Epilogue

Caitlyn curled her feet beneath her as she relaxed in the oversized chair in Pop Pop's sitting room. He'd moved into his own small living space in Riley's house on his eightieth birthday. The move had been precipitated by a tumble he'd taken while getting out of the bathtub. He'd lain on the cold tile floor for nearly two hours, unable to rise or call for help before Sean, who had stopped by for a visit, found him.

The episode had been upsetting enough—to him and his children—that they'd finally convinced him to move in with Riley. Killian, Sean and Justin had built an addition on Aaron and Riley's home, creating the perfect living space for Pop Pop. In addition to his bedroom and bathroom, he had a small sitting room that he referred to as his man cave. One wall was covered with a big flat-screen TV, and his well-worn, much-loved recliner sat right in front of it. There was also a comfy loveseat and the chair Caitlyn had claimed.

However, Caitlyn's favorite part of Pop Pop's man cave wasn't his collection of rare Pilsner glasses or his sports pennants. It was his wall of family pictures. Each member of the Collins clan was represented with one photo each. Pop Pop took great care in selecting his favorites, and when he found a photo he liked better, the old was swapped out for the new. As such, the wall was always changing, always offering something new to look at.

The only photo that never changed was the one in the very center of the wall, and it was Caitlyn's absolute favorite. It was a black-and-white picture of

Pop Pop and Grandma Sunday when they were dating and still living in Ireland. They were sitting together on an old stone walltogether. Pop Pop looked very dashing in a suit and tie—he'd told her once they'd been at his cousin's wedding—and Sunday was absolutely beautiful in her simple dress, a string of pearls around her neck. What always captured Caitlyn's attention, and held it, was the way Pop Pop and Grandma were looking at each other with complete and utterly unmasked love. It was as if they were the only two people on the planet.

Summer was approaching, and though they'd only been dating six months, Lucas was already dropping hints about marriage.

Okay, not necessarily hints. In fact, neon signs proclaiming his intentions wouldn't have been as obvious as he was. He'd asked her ring finger size and managed to drag her into three jewelry stores to inquire about what sort of rings she liked. She kept telling him it was too soon to start talking about marriage and weddings, but the fact was she couldn't quite convince herself that was true.

"Here we go," Pop Pop said when he walked back into the room. He'd invited her over this afternoon, proclaiming he had a surprise for her.

She sat up straighter as he walked toward her. She reached out to take the frame in his hand.

"Oh," she said when she saw the photo showcased behind the glass.

She hadn't seen the photo before, but she knew exactly where it had been taken. Two months earlier, they had opened the Collins House. There'd been a small celebration the day the first residents moved in. She and Lucas, along with several members of her family, had helped Moose move into his new—old—

place. They'd given him the same apartment, but the look on his face when he'd seen all the improvements had been exciting.

Then she'd caught sight of her Pop Pop and Moose wiping tears from their eyes, and she'd been hard-pressed not to shed a few tears of her own. Lucas had seen her reaction, and he'd stepped behind her, wrapping his arm around her to nuzzle her cheek affectionately. Bubbles had called out her name and snapped the photo.

She was looking at the camera, but Lucas...

Lucas was looking at her the same way Pop Pop had looked at Sunday all those years ago at a wedding in Ireland.

Pop Pop took the picture from her hands. "It's going on the wall."

"Lucas wants to marry me." She hadn't meant to blurt that out. She hadn't told anyone about it, still foolishly resisting the idea.

Pop Pop didn't show the slightest glimmer of surprise. "Of course he does. The man is crazy about you. So when's the wedding?"

"Pop Pop. Don't you think it's a bit soon in the relationship to start talking about marriage?"

He took her old picture off the wall, one in a series her aunt Natalie had taken in her studio for Caitlyn when she needed a professional photo done. Caitlyn had selected a more serious photo for work purposes. Pop Pop had, of course, opted for the one that had been an accident. Natalie had told her a funny story about Ewan, and Caitlyn had laughed. Natalie and Pop Pop had proclaimed that photo of her cracking up the best of the batch.

"Do you love Lucas?"

"You know I do."

"And he feels the same? He's good to you?"

She grinned, knowing perfectly well where he was going. "You know he does."

"Then marry him."

"That's it? Just marry him? I have to admit I'm sort of disappointed. Where's my story about you and Grandma? My wise words?"

Pop Pop chuckled, placing the photo of her and Lucas on the wall. "After all these years, I'd think you would be sick of my stories and old-man adages."

"Never," Caitlyn said with utter sincerity.

"Come here, Caitlyn."

She stood and crossed the room to him.

Pop Pop pointed to the photo of her and Lucas. "Do you know what I see when I look at that picture?"

Caitlyn studied the photo. "Love?"

"Yes, definitely. But more than that, I see my beautiful, lively, sensitive granddaughter. I see the brave Cathleen, who saved all the poor Irish from the devil."

Caitlyn laughed. "I forgot about Cathleen."

Pop Pop shook his head. "No, you didn't. She's been living in your subconscious since you were four years old. I've seen it. Watched as you've taken on countless cases that seemed impossible. Cases you went on to win because of your fearlessness as well as your endless supply of caring. You fight for the underdog."

"What does that have to do with me marrying Lucas?"

"Och. That should be obvious. You went to battle with the devil to save the Irish."

Caitlyn tilted her head. "Are you saying Lucas is the devil?"

"Isn't that what you believed? When he was trying to buy the pub, trying to sabotage us in order to steal it?"

Caitlyn reared back. "You knew about that?"

"I raised my kids to be honest. Because of that, they are terrible liars. Plus, I'm a nosy old man with too much time on his hands. I eavesdropped on that first meeting Lucas had with your mom, Ewan and Tris. Knew about the whole thing from the start."

"Why didn't you say anything?"

"Because I knew they wouldn't sell the pub. That place isn't just a business. It's our home."

"You're not clearing anything up for me, Pop Pop. In fact, I think I'm more confused."

"Don't you see? Not only did you save the Irish, my wee Cathleen, you saved the devil too. And now you aren't alone in your battles. Now you have a true and worthy partner, one who would walk through flames for you. Think of all the good the two of you can do together. Marry the lad and go save the world."

She looked at the picture of her and Lucas. Then she turned her attention to the one of Pop Pop and Sunday.

She'd always envied that love. Now, she felt it. Every single day she woke up next to Lucas. She was finished fighting, finished denying herself the happy ending she'd always dreamed up. She was claiming her devil once and for all.

"I love you, Pop Pop."

"And I love you, Caitie-bug."

Other books in the Wild Irish series

Come Monday

Wild Irish, Book One

Monday's child is fair of face...

After the death of her mother years prior, Keira Collins willingly put aside her dreams to become a surrogate parent to her six younger brothers and sisters. At twenty-seven, she's finally pursuing a college degree. Between classes, working at the family pub and still tending to siblings, she's no time for romance. So why is she spending all her rare free time fantasizing about hot Professor Wallace bending her over his desk?

Will Wallace recognizes Keira's unfulfilled desires, her habit of hiding her beauty, her obsessive need for control in every aspect of her life. But Will has needs of his own—and they run far darker than Keira's. As he initiates her into his lifestyle, offering sweet punishments and sweeter rewards, Will's sexual authority slowly strips away some of her precious control. The one thing Keira's not ready to relinquish...

Ruby Tuesday

Wild Irish, Book Two

Tuesday's child is full of grace...

Sky Mitchell is hiding out in Baltimore, seeking peace and solitude while he struggles with a career decision. Lead singer of popular rock group The Universe, he's thinking of going it alone. Wandering into an Irish pub, he's ecstatic to discover the breakout single for his solo album—but the songwriter doesn't want to sell. He challenges the woman to a contest. Not only does he win the song, but also a songwriting partner to complete the rest of the album.

Teagan Collins is sure of her talent but she's never aspired to fame and fortune. She's content singing folk tunes in her family's pub. Working on an album with Sky tests her patience…and her libido. The hot rocker plays her body like a fine instrument, their desire deepening with each song they write. But someone doesn't want Sky to go solo, and will stop at nothing to sabotage the couple's efforts. Undaunted, Sky wants Teagan to join him onstage at his farewell concert to sing her original, "Maybe Tomorrow"…

If they make it through today.

Waiting for Wednesday

Wild Irish, Book Three

Wednesday's Child is full of woe…

Tristan Collins knows Lane Bryce is strictly hands off. She's smart, funny, kind…and married. But he still looks forward to her once-a-week visits to the family pub where he tends bar. When she fails to arrive one

Wednesday, Tris is concerned. When he learns she's in the hospital, brutally beaten after attempting to leave her unhappy marriage, he's enraged. Tris vows to protect her, but he doesn't get the chance. Lane checks out of the hospital and disappears without a trace.

A year later, newly divorced Lane is back, and enjoying her independence too much to embark on a relationship. Tris intends to prove she can have freedom and love, and he's not above using seduction to do it. The more she resists, the more he sets her body ablaze with pleasure the likes of which she's never known.

After a lifetime of disappointment, trust doesn't come easily for Lane. But when her ex-husband reenters her life, threatening her independence, her happiness, she could discover too late that Tristan is the one man worthy of not only her trust, but also her love.

Sweet Thursday

Wild Irish, Book Four

Thursday's child has far to go…

In high school, Lily was too shy to do anything about her feelings for her best friends, Justin and Killian. Now she's ready to put to rest her regrets with a proposal that might shock even her oversexed friends— the three of them, together, one night, multiple positions.

K and J are more than a little surprised to see Lily at their ten-year reunion. The plain Jane they remember is now a stunning woman—who wants to have sex with both of them. Who are they to deny her? Even if Killian suspects they might be treading on dangerous emotional territory. The night stretches into the weekend and, as K suspected, none of them want it to end. But he and Lily know people live in pairs, not trios, and they call a halt now, before it's too late.

Justin, however, knows a good thing when he sees it. He's ready to fight for what he wants...what they all need. He just has to convince Lily and Killian that unconventional can also be extraordinary.

Friday I'm in Love

Wild Irish, Book Five

Friday's child is loving and giving...

Ewan Collins has had the hots for Natalie for years but she continually rebuffs him, supposedly because of their age difference. When Natalie comes to stay with the Collins family for a week, Ewan decides it's time to make his move in a serious way.

Natalie's been in a funk since celebrating another birthday alone. When Ewan proposes to help her "get a life"—seven lessons in seven days—she figures what the hell does she have to lose? Ewan's plans include tequila shots, fishing, karaoke...and other, more erotic hands-on demonstrations. But loneliness isn't Ewan's only obstacle. Tragedy in her past continually takes Natalie to a dark place her mind can't easily overcome.

With support, tenderness and love, Ewan plans to win over Natalie one lesson at a time. Starting with lessons of the heart.

Saturday Night Special

Wild Irish, Book Six

Saturday's child works hard for a living…

What do you get when you cross a gold-digging stripper, a down-on-her-luck hooker, an estranged husband, his knocked-up wife, a Wayne Newton lookalike taxi driver and one beleaguered Baltimore cop? A typical night in the life of Riley Collins—Vegas style. Riley's always been the wildest of the Collins clan, but even she bites off more than she can chew during an impromptu trip to Sin City.

Once again, it's Aaron Young to the rescue. No surprise; Aaron's been watching Riley's ass forever—and he's wanted to spank it for even longer. Tracking her down, Aaron finally gets his wish—after he drags a drunken Riley to a chapel and makes it legit, of course. To say she's shocked is putting it mildly. But Riley warms to Aaron's seduction quicker than you can say "all-you-can-eat buffet!" Who knew her mild-mannered best friend was so hot in the sack?

Of course, thanks to Riley's penchant for picking up strays, the newlyweds will have to sneak in some honeymoon boom-boom whenever they can. But they'll manage...

Any Given Sunday

Wild Irish, Book Seven

The child who is born on the Sabbath day, is bonny and blithe and good and gay.

Sean Collins is happy working at the family pub and sharing a house with the woman of his dreams. He and Lauren are equals in every way, including in bed, where they burn the sheets. Life is good. Even if he must hide a couple of secrets to keep it that way.

Lauren is madly in love with Sean. They share everything—almost. She can't deny sensing...something. A certain feeling when she, Sean and their friend Chad are all together. But she doesn't press. How can she when she's not being completely forthright herself?

Chad is feeling pretty miserable, and renting a room in Sean and Lauren's home has only made it worse. In a house filled with secrets, Chad's are doozies.

When an opportunity arises to explore their deep desires, the trio plunges into a sex-filled, emotionally charged ménage. Long-buried feelings are revealed, changing their lives irrevocably. Whether for better or worse, only Sean, Chad and Lauren can decide.

Wild Irish Christmas

Wild Irish, Book Eight

"To Conall Brannagh." Ewan took the bottle from his father. "Who?" "Conall Brannagh," Patrick repeated. "If your mother had chosen him over me, none of us would be here tonight."

It's Christmas Eve, and the Collins siblings have given their father a precious gift. All seven have gathered together to spend the night in his apartment above the family pub, the warm, loving home where Patrick and Sunday raised their large brood.

You've witnessed each child find their happy-ever-after. Now gather 'round the tree and join the Collins family as they pass a bottle of Jameson, and Patrick shares the story of how he won the heart of Sunday, his true love, his soul mate…and the mother of his seven Wild Irish.

ABOUT THE AUTHOR

Writing a book was number one on Mari Carr's bucket list. Now her computer is jammed full of stories — novels, novellas, short stories and dead-ends. A *New York Times* and *USA TODAY* bestseller, Mari finds time for writing by squeezing it into the hours between 3 a.m. and daybreak when her family is asleep.

You can visit Mari's website at www.maricarr.com. She is also on Facebook and Twitter.

Look for these titles by Mari Carr

Big Easy:
Blank Canvas
Crash Point
Full Position
Rough Draft
Triple Beat
Winner Takes All
Going Too Fast

Boys of Fall:
Free Agent
Red Zone
Wild Card

Compass:
Northern Exposure
Southern Comfort
Eastern Ambitions
Western Ties
Winter's Thaw
Hope Springs
Summer Fling
Falling Softly
Heaven on Earth
Into the Fire
Still Waters
Light as Air

June Girls:
No Recourse
No Regrets

Just Because:
Because of You
Because You Love Me
Because It's True

Lowell High:
Bound by the Past
Covert Affairs
Mad about Meg

Second Chances:
Fix You
Dare You
Just You
Near You
Reach You
Always You

Sparks in Texas:
Sparks Fly
Waiting for You
Something Sparked
Off Limits
No Other Way
Whiskey Eyes

What Women Want:
Sugar and Spice
Everything Nice

Trinity Masters:
Elemental Pleasure
Primal Passion
Scorching Desire
Forbidden Legacy
Hidden Devotion
Elegant Seduction
Secret Scandal
Delicate Ties
Beloved Sacrifice
Masterful Truth

Masters' Admiralty:
Treachery's Devotion
Loyalty's Betrayal
Pleasure's Fury
Honor's Revenge
Bravery's Sin

Cocktales:
Party Naked
Screwdriver
Bachelor's Bait
Screaming O

Wild Irish:
Come Monday
Ruby Tuesday

Waiting for Wednesday
Sweet Thursday
Friday I'm in Love
Saturday Night Special
Any Given Sunday
Wild Irish Christmas

Wilder Irish:
Wild Passion
Wild Desire
Wild Devotion
Wild at Heart
Wild Temptation
Wild Kisses
Wild Fire
Wild Spirit

Individual Titles:
Seducing the Boss
Tequila Truth
Erotic Research
Rough Cut
Happy Hour
Power Play
Assume the Positions
Slam Dunk